"Do what I say if you want to stay alive."

Ethan pushed her back into the convenience store. "Keep away from the windows. I'm going out. I'll let you know when it's safe."

"And then?"

"Just follow my orders and no one gets hurt." He hoped. The last time his orders were followed, a woman almost died.

He stepped out under the canopy. The helicopter's motor blasted his eardrums, and the smell of gasoline mixed with his own scent of fear. One peek and he could be riddled with holes. But what else could he do? Call for backup, he supposed. But he worried his backup was in the chopper, ready to take Roni in.

Or down.

A car screamed into the parking lot, but all Ethan could see was the gun pointed out the window. Three shots wrenched the air, none at him. He wished he'd been the target when he saw what the shooter aimed for. A propane tank beside the store.

Ethan knew what was coming. But he was too late to stop it.

Katy Lee writes suspenseful romances that thrill and inspire. She believes every story should stir and satisfy the reader—from the edge of their seat. A native New Englander, Katy loves to knit warm, wooly things. She enjoys traveling the side roads and exploring the locals' hideaways. A homeschooling mom of three competitive swimmers, Katy often writes from the stands while cheering them on. Visit Katy at katyleebooks.com.

BLINDSIDED

KATY LEE

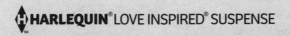

HARLEQUIN® LOVE INSPIRED® SUSPENSE

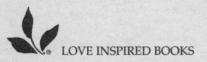

LOVE INSPIRED BOOKS

ISBN-13: 978-0-373-67764-1

Blindsided

www.Harlequin.com

Stand fast therefore in the liberty wherewith Christ hath made us free, and be not entangled again with the yoke of bondage.
—*Galatians* 5:1

He hath made everything beautiful in His time.
—*Ecclesiastes* 3:11

To Brianna, the daughter my heart chose.

Acknowledgments

I'm the safest driver you will ever find on the road, definitely a following-the-rules kind of gal. So all these speed chases had to be researched and yes, tried in a safe environment. I am thankful to the Rusty Wallace Racing Experience and Gotham Dream Cars for their expertise and training. Honestly, I have loved the thrill of getting behind the wheel of so many different kinds of cars, from a stock car to a Ferrari. The pressure against my head as the race car careens around a turn at 120 miles per hour is not something I ever would have thought about—and definitely would never do on my own. Kids, don't try this at home, either! But the experiences are out there to be had with organizations like Rusty Wallace and Gotham if you ever want to give it a whirl. Be safe. Drive safe. Enjoy!

ONE

Veronica Spencer's fuchsia patent leather boots, useless in the New Hampshire soggy spring, stalled on the backlot pavement of her racetrack. The sound of mechanical whirring and the clang of metal tools came from behind the closed bay doors of a dark, unused garage at Spencer Speedway. This was *her* garage, she silently staked her claim. She had a plan for it, and it didn't include a squatter.

The damp, cold, night wind matched her bitter mood and fluttered her signature rose pink silk scarf, also not an accessory for functionality— but in the case of her scarves, glamour wasn't their purpose either. Mutilated scar tissue from a car fire at three years of age covered her neck and right arm. It was the arm she'd used to reach for her mother, who'd sat in the front passenger seat before the flames killed her. Roni's burns reminded her of the memory daily. The scarves?

They helped her forget.

They also had a way of putting people at ease when they saw her coming. Gave them something pretty to look at instead.

Roni had no intentions of putting her intruder at ease.

She smiled the first smile since she left her uncle grumbling at his dining room table earlier that night.

Perhaps taking the scarf off to show this trespasser what ugly looked like would make him second-guess squatting on her track again for… what? Just what was he doing here this late at night when the track remained closed for the season? The sounds told her he was building a car. He probably planned to race it in the Icebreaker, the first spring race, next week.

Not a chance, buddy. Not on my track. And not anyone else's after the sponsors heard what Roni Spencer had to say about him. He wouldn't be the first man who underestimated her influence in the racing world.

The last one would never race again.

Her determined steps picked up, but at the door, deep, guttural voices filtered out and tripped her up again.

Someone gave an order like a drill sergeant breaking in new recruits, or more like threatening their lives. Her hand paused on the doorknob, and her gaze shot to the window a few feet to her left.

The square glass panes were covered with

black paper. From afar it appeared dark and un-used. Up close it all appeared...*criminal.* As much as she wanted to meet her trespasser face-to-face, perhaps barging in might not be the way to go. Her choice of weapon was her cutting tongue. Something told her she might not like theirs.

Always known for her uncanny ability to escape trouble, on and off the track, Roni grabbed her cell phone from the back pocket of her white jeans and backed away. Sometimes Reverse saved lives.

Her black Porsche Carrera beckoned at thirty feet where she'd parked it, and now with each retreating step she wished she'd pulled up closer. But that might have alerted the intruders to her presence if she had.

This wasn't the first time the track had seen il-legal activity. A few months back the main office had been ransacked, computers stolen, windows smashed. She loved her little town of Norcastle, but she knew it had fallen on hard times before; many were still struggling. It was only realistic that crime would follow. She wasn't naive. She was an intelligent businesswoman—despite what her uncle implied and what her ex-fiancé denied.

She'd approached her uncle Clay again tonight about opening a racing school at the track. And again, he'd scoffed. "No man will ever want to learn how to race from a girl. Especially one so... *pink*," he'd said. "Didn't you learn your lesson with Jared? Your own fiancé didn't want his peers knowing you were the brains behind his driving. Why would anyone else?"

Veronica punched in 911 with a vengeance. She'd handle this without calling Uncle Clay. She'd show him she could manage the run of the place without *anyone else.* He was free to leave his CEO position anytime. With her brother Wade retiring from the army and finally moving back to New Hampshire with his new wife, Lacey, Uncle Clay's days of being in charge since the car crash twenty-eight years ago that took her parents and baby brother, Luke, away from her were coming to an end.

Her thumb moved to the call button. Her decision to do this alone meant so much more to her than making a phone call. It meant independence.

But just as her thumb pressed the button, the phone disappeared from her hand. Just like that. One moment she held it in her grasp, the next it flew out into the night. Before she could fathom the occurrence, a yank on her scarf jerked her head back in a sharp, quick, painful snap. Roni's throat closed to life-giving air. She felt a body behind her, but the identity of her assailant took a backseat. In her struggle, her red hair whipped across her face like a red flag of warning that had come too late.

"You're in the wrong place at the wrong time, *chica.* Too bad for you." The harsh voice of the drill sergeant spoke close to her ear as his hand twisted the scarf tighter.

Gurgles escaped Roni's mouth, her long nails breaking as she clawed at her neck. *Useless*, her mind blared. But it also didn't give her any other ideas in its fog-laden, asphyxiating state. Her vision blurred even as she felt her eyes bulge with each painful twist of her scarf, tighter and tighter. Her only thought was when would the pain finally end? How long must she endure the torture? It was the same question she'd asked herself since she was three, when the agony of her burns consumed her, and then, when the sting of being marred for life set in. When would the pain end? The answer was always the same.

Never.

Was that the answer for her tonight?

Roni grappled with the material of her scarf. Her scars beneath would never go away. But Jared's success on the track under her tutelage these past couple of years had given her an idea. A hope.

The Roni Spencer School of Racing.

Roni had something to offer. She knew it now, and it was why she'd come to the garage tonight. There would be no more putting it off.

And she would not allow her dream to fall by the wayside along with her dumped body!

Roni bent her knees to drop her weight in a faux fall. Judging by the way her scarf pulled down, her choke holder stood shorter than her nearly six feet in heels. She used her tall frame against him. He would have to lift her or risk falling forward himself. As his knees bent, she brought a foot up and kicked back at him, heel first. In the dark, she could only hope she hit her mark.

His hold loosened and both of them fell to the ground, apart. Stunned, she continued to claw at her neck as air rushed back in. Her lungs heaved and spots brightened in her eyes, but she pushed her body to face her attacker before another attempt could be made. He got to his knees and spit. His hands shot out of the darkness for her.

Roni rolled away. She wished she could tell the loser he was messing with the wrong person, but her dented voice box blocked her sharp tongue. Anger surged within her. Had the man known her weapon of choice?

He reached for her again, and Roni kicked out. Her body flew back...right into an unmovable wall.

Her hand reached behind her. *No*, she realized, *not a wall*.

The legs of a second intruder blocked her. The solid mass of a strong-armed, muscled man in a black tank and unbuttoned white shirt towered over her. So much taller than the other guy...and so much bigger. She scooted to her right and crab-walked back, outnumbered and outwitted without her voice.

"What do you think you're doing?" the guy standing over her barked.

"Me?" Roni squeaked, her throat strained. Her hand fumbled on empty pavement in a last-ditch effort to find her phone. "You're on…my…property."

"I wasn't talking to you," he replied, his voice low and disgusted.

In the light of the moon, she watched her assailant step up to the tall, hulking man. She craned her neck to see them face off with each other.

"What does it look like I'm doing? Tying up loose ends, because *you* were sleeping on the job. Now get inside so I can finish it."

The tall man didn't make a move. Just crossed his arms at his chest. "You can't kill her. She's Veronica Spencer, the *owner*. Do you have any idea of the media frenzy you would cause? She's high profile. Her family wouldn't stop until they got you and every person who knows you."

"Well, she sure ain't walking out of this place. Now get inside."

Hanging around to see who won the battle wasn't Roni's style. She made a run for the moonlit outline of her Carrera, Spanish for *race* and *career*, but the loss of her career would be the least of her worries if she didn't get her feet in gear.

Her breath hitched with each rapid footstep,

one in front of the other. Her car closed in, her arms reached out. The door handle brushed her fingertips just as her scarred arm was yanked back in a vice grip. Instantly, her legs flew out in front of her as her body smacked hard into the shorter guy's chest.

He held her with both arms this time. She couldn't budge in any direction or with any part of her body. Her squirms and painful screams did nothing as he dragged her back to the garage.

"Open the door, Gunn."

"I told you, you can't kill her." It was the big guy talking. Would he help her?

"And you're not in charge. I am. You keep forgetting that."

She took that as a no.

Gunn opened the door as instructed, and Roni saw her first real glimpse of him as the short guy carried her over the threshold. Blond hair, curls at his nape and eyes that tripped her up. She went for Gunn's baby blues, demanding he look at her. *See me*, she wanted to say. *Look at me. I'm a person.*

Conflict resided in their depths, but no compassion.

He turned away, and she knew he would be of no help. What a waste of a handsome face, she thought. He obviously lacked brains in exchange for it.

Roni accepted her solo fight, but that would

mean coming up with some fast thinking on her part.

First off, who were these men?

Were they friends of Uncle Clay? It would explain their presence in her garage if it was her uncle who let them on the property. Uncle Clay may have fooled the rest of her family into believing his innocent spiel about his involvement in the car crash that killed her parents, but he didn't fool her. He knew more than he let on, and she wouldn't stop digging until she discovered everything.

But just how far would he go to stop her?

Would he invite criminals to her track to do his dirty work?

The door slammed behind Roni, cutting her off from the world and locking her inside with killers.

She craned her neck to see how many closed in on her. She swallowed past the burning pain in her throat and spoke as strong as she could muster. "You're not going to get away with this. I have family in the CIA." Not a total lie, just not sure if her grandfather could be contacted fast enough to save her. The man lived a secret life.

Her peripheral vision showed four men approaching, tools in their hands. Big metal crowbars and wrenches no doubt meant to silence her.

"You were saying?" The small but extremely

strong man holding her spoke into her ear, his breath hot and putrid.

Roni turned her face away to Gunn, the man who had saved her outside, *if* she could call it saving. In the full garage light, she thought his baby blues and blond curls warred against this whole lethal scene. He didn't look like the other guys with their shaved heads and tattoos etched into the sides of their necks, heads and arms. He also carried no wrench or any other tool to be used against her. But perhaps his weapon of choice wasn't of the visible kind.

No weapon formed against me shall prosper. The scripture popped into Roni's mind from someplace deep and forgotten. Cora had prayed it over her as a child, but it had been years since the Spencer family's maid had repeated the words. Roni had made it clear to Cora that when it came to God, she didn't want to hear about anything He had to say. But in these dire moments, Roni didn't question why His words came to mind now... only the fact that they brought on a sense of empowerment.

Power that she would need against these men.

They looked at her with such hatred. Maybe they weren't friends of Uncle Clay's, but of Jared's. That would really explain the flaming eye-daggers coming her way. Jared Finlay still sulked about her terminating their relationship.

Roni lifted her chin. Jared used her to jump-start his racing career. He got what was coming to him, exactly what he deserved.

And so would these lowlifes.

"What are you doing in my garage?" she demanded and glanced around the bays. Three vans, painted white, rear windows replaced with metal inserts to block the view to inside; car parts strewn about.

She had her answer but didn't want to believe it. Maybe she was wrong.

Yeah right, like these guys were legit.

"You're using my garage to clone cars?" she rasped angrily.

Car cloning was a federal offense. Stealing the identity of a legitimately owned vehicle and slapping it onto a stolen car in a chop shop gave the car a new identity so it could be used for criminal activity. Drug deals, mafia jobs, drive-by shootings, you name it. Criminals could get away with a lot when their cars didn't out them.

Roni sneered at the men. "How dare you use Spencer Speedway as your chop shop. I will not allow you to link my business to your crimes."

Gunn's eyes narrowed. His arms crossed at his front as they had outside.

"How did you know that's what we're doing here?" he said.

"I didn't, but thanks to your confession, I do now." She gave his formidable physique a quick once-over and continued, "Such a shame."

Roni's neck wrenched back in pain. Her original attacker grabbed her scarf again, tilting her head until she felt his prickly, unshaven cheek against her. "I should have killed you immediately, *chica*. You talk too much."

Something hard pushed into the side of her head.

It clicked.

Roni closed her eyes on a sharp inhale. This was how she would die? Shot down in her own garage. The place that was supposed to be where her dreams of a racing school came to fruition. This was so unfair. But then, when had her life ever been fair?

She looked at Gunn, standing in front of her. No concern showed on his face. It was as if he didn't care one way or the other if his partner pulled the trigger, even after he'd saved her outside. He stepped up close and lifted a strand of her hair in his finger. "Red."

"Good, you know your colors. Your mother must be so proud." If Roni was about to die, she wouldn't go out cowering.

Gunn stilled, expressionless. Not the reaction she'd hoped for, but if imminent death didn't deflate her nerve, Gunn's lack of emotion wouldn't either.

"You've got moxie," he said. "That's dangerous."

The shuffling steps of the other four men

drifted to her ears. They tapped their various tools against hands itching to use them. Roni's breathing picked up even as her chin lifted higher to defy them to come any closer.

"I say we ransom her," Gunn said with a smirk inches from her face. "Think of the money, boys. She'll bring a pretty penny." He let her strand of hair go after one more brush between his fingers. "Her family would pay out big."

The room went silent. Then a deep, sick laugh erupted from the man who held the gun to her head. Slowly, he released the fabric of her scarf, then the pressure of the gun upside her head disappeared.

"I like the way you think, muchacho," he said in her ear, then shouted, "Stuff her in the back of my van. We're movin' out…now."

"No!" she yelled, but eager, grubby hands grabbed at her from all sides. All hands except for those of the man who just saved her from being killed…again.

But now Roni knew why he'd saved her.

Money. The root of all evil. And this blond-haired, tough guy with his mocking baby blues was the evilest of them all.

He was also no dummy.

But his weapon of intelligence made him more dangerous than any crowbar the other men carried.

A greasy rag filled her mouth on a gag and her

hands were bound behind her. She screeched and twisted with all her might, but one against six proved her fight hopeless.

No, not hopeless, she decided, settling her eyes on Gunn. She made sure he knew he would be the one to pay for every atrocity inflicted on her, right down to each and every broken nail.

The next second a bag covered Roni's head, putting her into complete darkness. She took solace knowing she'd made her message clear. Like Jared, Gunn didn't know how ruthless she could be, and also like Jared, he would soon find out.

FBI agent Ethan Rhodes needed to figure out a way to contact his handler, Pace O'Malley. He had a mock ransom to set up...and *fast*. With every mile away he drove, the stakes of life-and-death increased and his investigation imploded. Ethan stole a glance at the passenger seat where the vicious Franco Guerra practically licked his chops every time the woman stuffed in the back of the van restarted her screeching. She went through bouts since the second hour of driving north began. Ethan couldn't believe she had a voice left after the first hour. She had to be so raw.

And scared.

Although you wouldn't know it by looking at her. Ethan had never met anyone so brash when a gun was held to their head. She was either really sure of her fighting skills, or she was crazy.

Or, Pace was right about her, and she was working with Guerra's boss.

Pace had enough on her to link her to the operation, and the way she knew they were cloning cars showed her knowledge about it. But something didn't sit right with Ethan.

Veronica Spencer couldn't be a part of the organization, no matter what her bank statements read. Guerra had aimed his gun at her head and meant to kill her. Why, if they were cohorts?

Did the woman know how close to death she'd been in that moment? Ethan doubted it by the way she'd lambasted them all for being in her garage. She had been fearless, even after nearly losing her life in the parking lot. Franco had been torturing her then, cutting off her air little by little to prolong her misery, playing with her like a cat and its dinner.

Ethan's lips curled in disgust. The man was beyond sick. Eight months of getting close to him had turned Ethan's stomach multiple times a day. The man had no loyalty to any of his men, using them as an example to the others when they "disappointed" him. One wrong move, and it was over. One guy caught with a cell phone a few months back paid the ultimate price when the phone nearly led the cops to Guerra's door. Ethan didn't dare have a cell on his person, which meant he was deep under with no contact with his handler. Just a tracker in his boot and a gun on his ankle.

When Guerra's gun targeted the redheaded spitfire, Ethan knew Guerra would pull the trigger and laugh for days after. But what could be done to stop it, other than blowing the investigation?

Still Ethan had to try.

He had stepped up to her, planning to confiscate the gun and turn it on Guerra, but instead he said the first thing that came to his mind. The word *ransom* spilled from his lips. The only other thing Guerra liked more than torturing people was money. Veronica Spencer was worth a huge chunk of change. But still, as Ethan threw out the idea to ransom her, his lungs seized as he waited for Guerra's response. He thought for sure his cover was blown. A year's worth of going deep, tanked. An innocent woman's life, ended.

No. Not innocent. Ethan had to believe the evidence Pace had on the glamour girl. Enough to put her away for years. There were even pictures from a street race in Miami with her and Guerra. And as soon as Ethan could get her "ransomed" out of here, Pace could cuff her, and Ethan could get back to bringing down Guerra's ring—and the man he worked for.

As much as Franco Guerra was a despicable man, he wasn't the man Pace wanted. Guerra was a car thief and mechanic, a means to much more sinister crimes that his cloned vehicles contributed to.

The man waiting for the cars was the real prize.

Ethan had no name at this point, just the term Guerra used: the Boss.

The Boss was in charge of a whole list of crimes, but it was what he transported in these vans that was beyond comprehension. Drugs, yes, and lots of them. But apparently, the Boss didn't get the memo that the slave trade had ended. He trafficked thousands of victims in and around the United States each year, and Ethan had finally worked his way up to being one degree away from taking down one of the largest human trafficking operations in the States.

So close he was to cracking this case and infiltrating the operation successfully. So close he was to breaking free thousands of victims by putting away their owner.

So close.

The woman screeched again, an earsplitting sound, a reminder that he had another person to break out of here first. Get Veronica Spencer out before the whole investigation went down.

And if he could, do it without giving himself away.

She kicked the rear door for the hundredth time, and Guerra laughed with delight. "The *chica*'s got fire in her. I look forward to snuffing it out."

Ethan's stomach clenched along with his teeth. He fought the urge to pull over and arrest the sleazy man right there. Instead, he smiled Guerra's way and hoped that it covered his true feelings well.

As well as his growing doubts in Roni Spencer's guilt.

If she was working for the Boss like Pace said, why would Guerra try to take her out? A little disagreement between accomplices? Jealousy?

Or was this whole scene staged, made to look as if she was innocent in front of...who?

Him?

Ethan sent a quick look Guerra's way. Had the man figured out he had an agent in his presence?

Ethan's hand curled tight around the steering wheel. "Are you going to give me some directions, or are we just going to drive all night?" he asked, acting as if he didn't really care.

"The Boss wants us to bring our feisty *chica* to him. He also wants to meet you. He was impressed with your vision to go big and ransom the woman. You just earned your way into the big house. What do you think of that?"

Ethan's saliva glands juiced. He could taste the victory with this case already. *So close* had just become *right now*.

Ethan envisioned the win being handed to him

on a silver platter, although knowing the extent of this ring, the platter would be solid gold. He couldn't wait to tag the platter as Asset Forfeiture, and every other piece of property stolen by this crime ring. If he believed God cared one bit about him he might have thought he was being handed the win as some sort of reward. But that couldn't be the case. God would never give him anything. And Ethan definitely didn't deserve a reward, nor did he want any favors. He'd learned it was best never to expect any, especially in his line of work. He had a job to do, and he did it alone. Period.

Ethan switched lanes and answered Guerra's question with an aloof shrug. "Should be interesting, but I was looking for some pocket change. I thought we were going to ransom the woman. What could the Boss possibly want with Spencer?"

Guerra stilled and glared at him with his beady black eyes. The man didn't appear to buy Ethan's nonchalance.

Ethan readied to spring into fight mode, his gun within reach in his ankle holster.

"Remember, muchacho, I'm putting my life on the line by bringing you along. I could leave you right here, if you catch my drift."

Ethan locked his eyes on Guerra's black-gazed warning. Slowly, Ethan smirked as if to say, is this a joke? A slow rumble of a laugh erupted from his tight vocal cords. The bluff was a risk, but no fear could be shown or he would be pushing up this spring's daisies along the roadside.

Guerra smirked in return and chuckled, too, at first low, then loud and cackled. A laughing hyena came to mind, all sharp teeth bared in a wide-open mouth; 100 percent vicious and sickly illuminated by the lights of the dashboard. "The Boss is going to like you, Ethan Gunn. Keep heading north. We're going to the border. Right outside Canada in a logging community. The middle of nowhere, really. Wait till you see this place. Our *chica* might never want to leave, *if* she even could."

Ethan stilled his hands on the wheel. Once again Guerra's words didn't sit right. "And we'll ransom her there?"

"We'll see," Franco said with a small smile and looked out his window. End of conversation.

Again, Roni Spencer felt like a victim in all this, not an accomplice. She felt like an innocent civilian caught up in his investigation.

Ethan bit down on the inside of his cheek, remembering the last civilian he'd snagged in an investigation—and nearly got killed. He'd vowed never again. Solo or no-go. That's how it had to be with him.

Ethan peered into the rearview mirror to the woman tied up in the back. Not a noise or movement could be heard now. He doubted she'd fallen asleep. She had to be listening to them. Had Guerra's words ground her impudence into fear? Was she feeling as sick as he was? He had to stop this from going any further.

"I don't think we should be bringing her," Ethan said. "She doesn't seem the type to go quietly. She could get us all killed."

"Boss's orders, and what he says, goes. I don't think you want to get on his bad side. And not mine either. Now drive." Guerra put his gun on his lap, his trigger finger itching to make his point.

Ethan continued north and thought of his tracking chip sewn into the inseam of his boot. He trusted Pace to be charting his every move north and following with the team. They wouldn't be too far behind and would be ready to move in with guns blazing if Ethan needed them. But only if. Anything earlier would jeopardize the investigation, and Pace wouldn't make his move a moment too soon.

Ethan drove on, leading Pace to the Boss, but that also meant leading Roni Spencer into even more danger. Whether she was a criminal or civilian didn't matter.

He shot another look in the rearview mirror. The bundle on the floor remained still and quiet. Regardless of what Pace believed about her, something told Ethan he'd just graduated from undercover car thief in this operation to nefarious human trafficker. And Roni Spencer was his first delivery.

TWO

Roni's aching head took hit after hit as the van bounced over a deep-rutted road. Logging roads in the middle of nowhere. They'd left the smooth highways a while ago and traveled far enough from her home that none of her family would ever find her. Not the one in the CIA, and not even Wade's intelligent service dog, Promise.

The van thumped again and Roni forced her eyelids closed, swapping the tormenting darkness of her shroud for a darkness she controlled. Her arms and legs had long gone numb from the constricting ropes bound to her appendages. They drove her to near insanity, but not as much as her fear. In this moment of stark terror, all she wanted was her mom.

The image that formed in Roni's mind wasn't one of the photographs that portrayed her birth mother, but instead, a living and breathing woman, Cora Daniels, came to mind.

Cora was so much more than the family's maid.

She had worked for the Spencers long before Roni was born. It was Cora who cared for Roni so lovingly after the loss of her parents. It was Cora who filled the role as mother through the many surgeries on Roni's burns and through the emotional pain that followed for so long after. It was Cora who made sure Roni never felt left behind, not when her parents died and not when Wade left for the army. Cora was Roni's support team when her blood relatives weren't, when her own uncle— her guardian—found her lacking. Roni pushed thoughts of Uncle Clay away. She didn't need his negativity in her moment of life-and-death. She refocused on Cora's loving face in her mind.

As long as she had Cora by her side, Roni pushed on. A life without her would be unbearable.

Cora's last conversation with her that morning at breakfast filtered in. She'd brought up retirement again. Roni shook it off just as she had that morning.

Every time Cora brought it up Roni would cover her ears and sing "You Are My Sunshine" out loud. It had been their song since the day Roni woke up in the hospital wrapped in gauze. Only then it had been Cora singing because it would be a long time before Roni felt well enough to sing, or talk, or even whisper.

The van took a sharp right and came to a

screeching halt, jamming Roni against the side wall. There was nothing Cora could do for her now. These men were killers, and the only way she would survive would be to play by the rules until a ten-second window opened up. Ten seconds would be all she needed to make her getaway.

The rear van doors creaked open and harsh hands pulled her out, feetfirst. Her covering was lifted off her head, exposing the two main criminals from her garage.

Her gaze caught the baby blues, and she dismissed their owner with a turn of her head.

"Time to meet the Boss, *chica*," said the short, vicious one. He whipped the gag out of her mouth. "Don't bother screaming. No one will hear you out here." He tossed a head to reference the thick black forest around her.

She'd been taken to the middle of nowhere. On a sigh, she nodded her acceptance to remain silent and Gunn untied her feet to allow her to walk. Compliance would lead her to that window of escape. Except when she came around the van, the sight before her halted her in her tracks.

"What's the matter, *chica*? Never seen a castle before? This one comes complete with a dungeon." He pushed her toward a solid stone structure and her hope threatened to wane.

So much for windows.

* * *

Ethan walked behind Roni Spencer, his senses on full alert. Were Pace and his backup crew far behind? Would they arrive before the trio entered this stone monstrosity? He listened for them, but the only sound he heard was Roni's boots clicking on the cobblestones. His men would know something was up when Ethan's tracker alerted them to his moving away from the racetrack and Norcastle. Without a phone call to say why, they would swoop in. Ethan braced for the deluge of FBI agents that he hoped would make their move before the towering entrance doors closed behind them. His hand flexed for the moment he would retrieve his gun from the holster at his ankle and join in. His heart raced with the anticipation of finally taking Guerra down. Ethan would make sure he missed the grass and hit the cobblestones when he did.

As soon as Pace saw Roni was here, he would go after her with cuffs. Ethan knew it even without a briefing. His handler didn't like the woman and itched to take her down. If Ethan didn't know better, he would think there was something personal between the two, but then, the woman was getting richer off the organization and Pace had been working this case for years. Ethan couldn't fault his friend for being disgusted with the whole organization and anyone involved. But he also couldn't allow the man to mistreat Roni when he took her in. She didn't deserve that. She deserved…what? Fairness?

The evidence said otherwise.

But the idea of her face slammed up against the stone walkway beside Guerra's had Ethan stepping up close behind her. And just like that he made the decision to let Pace take down Guerra instead. A year of anticipation of doing the job himself flitted away on the basis of protecting this woman. Pace would say he'd gone soft. Him, Ethan Rhodes, an ex-hoodlum from South LA whose absentee father had hardened him to granite, soft. He scoffed.

Franco whipped around. "Problem, Gunn?"

Ethan stretched his fingers to make a grab for his holstered weapon. Staying undercover was crucial until his men made their appearance. If he blew it now, he wouldn't be the only one dead. There were others working this ring from other places. Corrupt nail salons, massage parlors, even country clubs. The message would be out that the investigation was compromised. The runners of the business fronts would retaliate, and the FBI agents working them would pay. Not to mention, the whole investigation would be botched and back to square one.

Ethan gave his uncaring shrug. "No problem. Just amazed at the elaborate digs the Boss has."

Guerra's snarl turned to an agreeing smile under the spotlights beaming down on them and most likely recording their every word. Ethan looked forward to confiscating the surveillance to see who else had come through these doors in the past. He wouldn't stop until this whole out-fit—and everyone a part of it—was disassembled. He looked at the back of Roni's black leather coat, her long silky hair cascading down it, and thought whatever it took, he would deliver…even her.

The huge wooden door ahead of them opened slowly on silent hinges. A man dressed in a black suit with jet-black hair waited on the other side. He stood tall with his arms down in a relaxed pose. The cavernous room behind him displayed the heads of elk and bear. Ethan judged the bear to be a grizzly but didn't dare take his eyes off the man to be sure.

"Bring her into the light," the man ordered. Franco went to push Roni forward, but she stepped up willingly.

Too willingly, Ethan thought. Was there any fear in the woman at all?

Or maybe her involvement was more than opening her track to the organization. Maybe she'd been here before. Would he find her on the surveillance?

Ethan gave a last hooded search to the tree line. *Anytime, boys,* he thought. But no hint of backup didn't mean they weren't out there. He trusted his team to show up when he needed them most.

The man at the door said, "Veronica Spencer, is it?"

Ethan perked an ear for the direction of the conversation in front of him. It would determine his next move. If things went south his gun would be coming out with or without backup.

"Yes. I'm Veronica Spencer." Roni lifted her chin, her voice clear of any hesitation.

"You're very pretty."

Ethan couldn't see Roni's face as he waited for her response...which didn't come.

So, flattery was all it took to silence Roni Spencer's tongue? Fancy that.

The man pressed in close to her, and Ethan moved up, as well. The guy lifted a hand to her hair. Ethan spread his fingers to make ready for a grab.

"I said, you're very pretty. Has anyone ever told you that?"

She shrugged. "Sure, but I never believed it."

The man smiled from one side of his mouth. "Let me assure you, you are."

"Oh, well, if you assure me, then it must be true."

Sarcasm. Thick as the wood beams holding this cavern up.

Ethan stifled a cough. Was the woman blind to the danger? Why would she throw the man's compliment back in his face?

If this was the Boss, Roni could have just

signed her death warrant. If the woman kept this up, Ethan figured saving sand from slipping through his fingers would be easier than keeping her alive.

The silence in the room thickened as the man studied her face. Her response confounded him just as much as it did Ethan.

Was this even the leader of the organization? Or another scout?

The man cleared his throat. "I've arranged a room for you upstairs. You'll find it comfortable…and what you're accustomed to, I'm sure."

So the guy knew who he had. Maybe that would help Ethan keep her alive.

"I don't plan to be here long," she said flippantly.

Ethan fisted his hands and pressed his lips. Oh, why couldn't this woman be the docile type?

A scar at the corner of the man's eye ticked. Ethan willed Roni to pick up on the fine line she pushed against. The guy leaned in closer and so did Ethan, ready to remove Roni from his reach.

"Is that right? Was I wrong to show you hospitality, then?" he asked with eyebrows raised to the high wood-paneled ceilings.

"No, you will be compensated accordingly, sir," Roni replied. "I can promise you that."

The man's brown eyes darkened; his jaw clicked. He looked to Franco Guerra with a snarl. "Guerra, I will see you in my office. Now."

Guerra dropped his gaze with his nod. The response from the car thief spiked Ethan's curiosity. Never had Ethan seen Franco drop his gaze to anyone.

Ethan's heart picked up its pace, even as he set his face to be void of emotion. It wasn't fear he checked. It was pure joy. He was in, and he'd found the mark. Or "the Boss" as Guerra called him, the head of the whole organization.

The heavy door slammed behind Ethan, echoing through the gaudy monstrosity funded by crime and jolting him back to his role here.

A young maid stepped out from behind a closed door, her head bent so low only the top of her silky black hair showed. Guerra cowered off like a leashed dog to the rear of the hall, and Ethan took a step to follow the men. Then two guards who were obviously packing heat followed the maid out into the hall and nodded to Roni to move up the stairs with them.

Ethan took a last look at the backs of Guerra and the Boss. He had a decision to make: find the evidence to take this crime ring down, or stay by Roni's side and protect her with his life.

He took the stairs. Mutters beneath his breath denied he was going soft.

Pace's voice in his head protested otherwise.

Roni's jail cell gleamed with expensive golden decor likely imported from around the world. The white sateen feather blanket on the canopied bed looked luxurious and comfortable.

She avoided finding out.

The beauty of the room juxtaposed with the ugliness of her captivity made her blind to her surroundings' appeal. No matter the extravagance, the room was still a jail cell.

Roni scanned the space for possible exits and cameras. She figured at least one guard stood out in the hall, if not more. Big Brother was watching. She cringed at the feeling.

So far her compliancy kept her from whatever nightmare was below the first floor. Could it really be a dungeon in the accurate sense of the word? Who built dungeons these days? Then again, who built castles?

Her own town of Norcastle had an old castle situated on top of the mountain, but it had been built by an eccentric relative of an English duke who moved to America nearly two hundred years ago. The building was now a historic landmark for tourists and hikers to climb to during the summer months.

But this place was different. A newly built replica of a medieval fortress designed for the sole purpose of flaunting wealth.

But wealth from what? she wondered. What exactly did the owner, "the Boss" as she overheard Guerra call him in the van, do to earn all this?

More importantly, how much money would

appease him for her ransom if he had such extravagance already?

Roni approached the vanity. A three-way mirror caught her multiple reflections at different angles. Her gaze went to her scarf. From one side, her scars hid beneath the fabric. But not on her right. The right side had a way of peeking out. Jared reminded her of this whenever they were together. She made the adjustment to rectify it just as he would have. In this case, she would have let him. Something told her she had to make the Boss believe she was worth every penny he demanded from her family.

She wondered if they'd been notified yet and absently rubbed her fingers over the fabric of the chair.

"Mulberry silk," she mumbled when the unique texture stole her attention. The finest and softest silk in the world. She would know after testing them all around her neck. She also knew it to be the most expensive and, at its exorbitant price, she'd passed on it for something less pretentious.

But this guy had furniture made with the stuff.

Again, her captor did not need her family's money. He had his own. And a lot more than she'd ever seen.

So then, what did he want? Why was she here?

A soft knock came, and Roni heard the lock click over. She straightened up to receive whoever was about to enter.

"Come in," she said, as if she had the authority to say otherwise.

Roni expected her captor, but when the door opened, the young woman who had led her upstairs returned with satin-tied bundles of linens, her head of black hair bowed as she entered without a sound. The girl hadn't said a word to Roni before and didn't appear to want to talk now as she walked to the bathroom. With the main door wide, Roni stepped up to look down the hall, ready to make a run for it.

But just as she noticed the hall clear on one side, Gunn filled the doorway with his massive build and stopped her. The man was a boulder, sharp contours and all, and she would be going nowhere with him as her guard.

"Just checking the accommodations," he said, looking beyond her into her room. "I see you even have your own maid."

"There's also no windows, so you don't have to worry about me making a break for it," she spouted back. "Has my family been notified about my ransom?"

"Not yet. Is there another exit from the room? Through the bathroom, maybe?"

"I already told you there's no way out." She crossed her arms at her front.

"I was thinking more along the lines of someone getting in. But just in case, I'll be right outside your door. Count on it." Then he leaned in, his clean-shaven jaw brushing her cheek, and she nearly jumped back from the shock he gave. "I'm going to get you out of here," he whispered against her ear, but she barely registered his words. Frustrated with the light-headed response his closeness caused, she shoved him away from her.

"So you can take the ransom for yourself? I wouldn't go anywhere with you." Roni slammed the door closed on his face and took delight in having the last word. Then the lock clicked back over, taking even that away from her.

On a huff, she checked herself before she turned to face the young girl. The maid stood by the bed, her head still bowed, but the bedcovers had been pulled back.

"Hello," Roni said, hoping the girl would engage.

She only nodded in reply. Her lashes blinked, a seemingly nervous reaction to Roni's greeting.

"Did I say something wrong?" Roni asked.

A low reply came. "They don't like us talking. Only working. I can help you get ready for bed now."

"Who's *us*? You and me?"

The girl shook her head. "Other girls. Please, senorita, let me help you. I can't be gone too long."

Roni ignored the plea in her voice. Something

felt off in this already off place. "There're more girls like you? How many?"

"My counting is not so good. And the number, it…it changes."

"Changes? Because girls quit?" Roni would have to think the turnover was pretty high in this warped place.

The girl's silky hair swished side to side with the shake of her head, but no answer came. Instead she peered out from behind her hair at the corner of the room as though someone watched. A wave of nausea swept over Roni. The picture of captivity this girl painted for her had all the details Roni needed to put two and two together—and what it meant for her. The owner's earlier compliment of her beauty sickened her even more. Guerra and Gunn had paraded her in here like some horse to be put on the auction block. "They have no intention of ransoming me, do they?"

The girl shrugged again and lifted her chin a bit. Roni caught her first glimpse of her youthful face and too-sad eyes before she dropped them again.

The kind of business the owner of this place ran became evident.

Human trafficking.

"What's your name?" Roni asked, fighting a surge of anger.

"You can call us *sirvientas*."

"Servant girl? I don't think so." No big surprise the girl wouldn't be called by her name. Her captors knew how to make her forget she was a person with an identity. "I'll call you by your name only. So what is it?"

She tilted her head in uncertainty. "I used to be called Magdalena."

"Then that is what I will call you."

"No." She raised her chin a little farther. "Magdalena is...gone."

The young girl's sad eyes had seen too much. Roni could spit nails, but that wouldn't help this young woman and who knew how many more there were.

"Then how about I call you Maddie. Will that be all right?"

The girl nodded with a twitch of a smile. The smile quickly vanished.

"My name is Veronica, but my friends call me Roni. So you can call me Roni, too."

Roni stepped up to the girl but dared not touch her. Her scars weren't visible like Roni's, but they were there just the same.

"Will you tell me how you got here? Were you taken like me?"

Maddie frowned. "I come from a village in Mexico. My mother, she was very sick, but we were too poor for medicine. A woman came and promised her I would marry a rich, handsome man if I go with her to work. She said she had a job for me. She was speaking our language. My mother trusted her. The woman paid my mother enough for medicine, and I went with her. We drove for a long time. A lot of hills went by. She brought me to a house and left me there. The man there, he pay her money before she go." Maddie dropped her chin to her chest and finished, "After she left, I knew my mother made a bad choice."

Silence ensued. "When was this, Maddie?"

"I'm nineteen now. I was sixteen."

"So three years you have been held captive, forced to work for no money." There was no sense asking her if that was true. It was obvious this wasn't a job.

A knock on the door broke their conversation. The lock clicked, but when it swung wide, it wasn't Gunn this time. It was the owner of this place. Roni curled her fingers into her palms. Never had she wanted to punch someone more. Not even Jared when he admitted to using her to spike his racing career. Not even when he checked to make sure her scarf covered her neck every time they entered the Winner's Circle to be photographed.

"*Sirvienta!* What is taking so long? You should be gone by now." The owner spoke fast, his skin taut over his clean-shaven cheeks, his black hair unmoved by his outburst.

Roni stepped in front of Maddie. "It's my fault. I was being chatty."

The man's jaw ticked, but after a second of staring over Roni's shoulder at Maddie's dropped head, he nodded once and gave Roni his full attention. "There's no chatting here. Don't forget you are a prisoner."

Maddie made her way to the exit, but Roni knew she couldn't let her go. "*Sirvienta*, I really need your help with…with finding some things before… I go to sleep for the night."

Maddie paused for direction from her master.

After a few seconds, he walked to the door, fury in his every step. "I'll see you in the morning, Miss Spencer. In the light of day, you'll see your future is really quite limited."

The door shut and clicked over. One look at Maddie's sad eyes and Roni knew she was just as trapped as this young woman.

She had to get out. Tonight, if possible.

Roni grabbed the chair to sit. Her hand grasped the Mulberry silk and the smooth material repulsed her. "I'm not going to bed, Maddie, but I do need your help." She glanced around the room and mouthed, "To escape. And you're coming, too."

Maddie's sad eyes sparked with what could only be her last shreds of hope. The innocent girl was still in there somewhere. Whatever tactics Maddie used to save herself from fully disappearing had worked.

Still, the spark died out with the shaking of

her head back and forth. "Oh, Roni, not me, but I do want to help you. It would mean so much to me, but how?"

Roni pushed a pad of paper and pen toward the girl, then whispered, "Draw me directions to where the Boss keeps his cars. I'll take it from there."

THREE

A guard in a black suit stood at his post by the Boss's office. From the stairway, Ethan watched around the corner as the guard read an incoming text on his phone. Ethan held his breath to see if an alert had gone out about him being missing from his post by Roni's room. As soon as Roni's guard took the maid down to the basement, Ethan made his way up the stairs to the top floor—the floor with the Boss's office.

Entrance into that office was critical. And so was time. Roni would only be safe for so long locked up in her room. He had to figure out how to get her out of this place, but first he needed to get an ID on who the Boss really was. Ethan needed a name, something Pace could use to hold the guy on while they ramped up the trafficking charges.

Ethan knew his team was out there, ready to move in, but would hold off until they had evidence in hand. Rushing in would only botch all their work.

The guard's phone rang. He answered on the first ring. "Yeah, I've got time. Boss is visiting a lady friend for the night." He shared a laugh with whomever was on the other end. Ethan wondered at the identity of the lady friend. Had the Boss left the premises to visit her? Or was the lady friend already in residence?

Roni?

She couldn't be the lady friend, Ethan thought as he looked down the stairway. One floor down was her locked-up-tight room. She was safe inside. He'd made sure of it.

Except the Boss would have a key.

Ethan needed to speed up this quest and return to her to see if she had unwanted company.

But first, he needed to access that office, so he could get Roni out for good. Too much was at stake, and for the first time in a year, it wasn't just the case.

Ethan waited for the guard to turn away so he could move in for a sneak attack, but the guard started heading in his direction. With his phone to his ear, the man said, "It's not my job to watch him. Guerra brought the guy in, he should be the one playing hide-n-seek with Gunn."

So the alert had gone out. He was a wanted man. And the guard was headed his way. The only way to go was back down.

Ethan took the steps in double time and launched his body over the railing at the bend. He shimmied down the spokes and held tight and still, breath and all.

The guard ran past him from above, never looking over the railing at the man hanging between the landings.

As soon as the guard made it to the lower floor, he turned the corner to continue down to the next one, saying, "I'll check the basement out. We don't need him snooping down there."

Ethan pulled his body up the railing spokes and over the railing. He hit the stair treads on a run and took the turn to the Boss's office. Ethan slipped inside and closed the door on a soft click. The computer sat off to the right side on a mahogany desk. He would start there.

The monitor hadn't gone to full sleep mode yet from when the Boss left. Having to come up with passwords would have slowed Ethan up. In reality, it would have stopped him in his tracks.

He opened an email account, but no names were listed on the account or any of the few emails in the in-box. Somewhere a name would have to be linked to the account. He clicked the trash files and waited for a couple of dozen to download.

With one eye on the screen, Ethan opened drawers and felt the numerous paperweights lined up on the desk front. They were substantial pieces, some sharp, some blunt. The Boss's weapons of torture, perhaps? Or death if things didn't go well for his victims. Ethan was pretty sure a blood scan over them would glow blue.

He picked up a heavy carving of a bull. It was some sort of trophy for the Most Valuable Player for a sports team. The name of the recipient had been scratched out. Figures the Boss thought of everything. But Ethan was counting on someone from his past not knowing him as the Boss. Someone who might email him with salutations to his real name.

Ethan tipped the bull trophy over and saw a compartment had been cut into its base. He slid the bottom cover off to find a single key.

The computer bleeped at its download end. He gave the deleted emails his full attention and found what he was looking for. Lyle Ramsey was the recipient name a sender used to forward some crass email joke.

"Well, hello there, *Lyle Ramsey*. Does your friend know what you do for a living?"

Ethan brought the computer back to the way he found it. He got what he'd come for. The processing team would take the PC when they were inside, but Ethan doubted they would find any evidence on it. Lyle didn't get to be the Boss by leaving a paper trail. And no paper trail meant cash houses. Find the cash houses and Lyle goes bye-bye. Ethan didn't think he'd have to look much further than the basement.

He picked up the phone and checked it for a dial tone. He dialed the secure number for Pace and said two words.

Lyle Ramsey.

Pace would know what to do with that.

Ethan hesitated to mention Roni's presence. A part of him didn't want Pace knowing she was with him. He knew what Pace would say to that.

"Do your job."

Ethan sighed and quickly relayed the message that Roni Spencer was in his custody. He clicked off just as voices filtered down the hall.

"If you brought some snitch into my house, you will pay, Guerra." The Boss's irate, booming voice echoed through the closed door.

"Gunn's not a snitch, but he does have high expectations for your average gofer. I've reminded him many times who's in charge. Something tells me he would push me aside if it got him ahead. If he wasn't so clever in his thefts, I would have wasted him months ago."

Ethan looked for a coat closet to hide in. He tried the door to his left.

Locked.

He circled the room. The drapes wouldn't hide his big frame. Nor would the cubby under the desk. He pulled the doorknob again, but it wasn't budging.

Then he remembered the key.

Guerra continued out in the hall. "The man's a

chameleon. Gets the job done before anyone sees a thing. Good at hiding out, which is why I can't find him right now."

The doorknob turned just as Ethan inserted the key and turned his own doorknob. He was behind the door, safely hidden from sight before Guerra and Ramsey entered the office.

But if Ramsey was here, what happened to the visit with his lady friend?

Was she in the office with them now?

Ethan turned to his side to listen with one ear, straining to make out another person's presence. Out of the corner of his eye, he noticed an elevator behind him. It would seem Ramsey had a private line down to the basement.

"And what about the Spencer woman?" Ramsey asked, his chair squeaking as though he leaned back into it. "What does she know?"

"Nothing. She thinks she's been kidnapped for her money and is here to be ransomed. I would have killed her at the garage, but Gunn stepped in. She can be disposed of now. Her family won't be expecting her home."

"Why's that?"

Ethan pressed his ear to the door, wondering the same question.

"As far as they're concerned their glamorous debutante was in the car theft business. The FBI is ready to close in. She'll go down for everything. All roads lead to her. When she disappears, everyone will believe she escaped to the Mediterranean to live on the run for the rest of her life."

"Everyone?"

Guerra laughed. "Well, not everyone. Someone paid me dearly to make her go away. I got the call to expect her tonight. That's how I knew to be looking for her before Gunn spotted her."

Ramsey chuckled. "I'm not surprised she angered someone enough to arrange her disappearance. She's strong-willed. I'd keep her here, but she's too tough to break. There's a reason I tell my scouts to go for the girls who can't look up. I tell them to flatter the girls. Tell them they're pretty. It's such a simple way to start, but oh, so effective. The girls who look you in the eye and say, 'Thank you' are the ones you pass on by. It's the girls who don't believe the compliments that become my inventory."

"When you told the Spencer woman she was pretty she didn't do either," Guerra pointed out.

"I know." Ramsey's voice held irritation. "That's why she needs to go."

"So what's the plan? Do you want me to go kill her? Or do you want to try your hand at breaking her?"

"Neither. I have someone else who will gladly take her. My connection who runs the outfit in Greece. He likes redheads, and I owe him a favor."

Ramsey went on to talk about a new shipment

coming in, but Ethan's mind blared with the realization that his instincts had been right about Roni. She really *was* innocent, and if he didn't get her out of here, she would disappear forever.

Ethan grabbed the doorknob, ready to do whatever had to be done to stop what these men planned. But to run out there now would only get himself killed before he could save her from a worse demise.

But if Guerra was telling the truth, then her home wasn't safe for her either. Someone she knew and trusted wanted her dead.

If Ethan called in his team right now, Pace would cuff her for sure. She wouldn't be safe with his men either. Pace was wrong about Veronica Spencer, though. She was the fall guy. Roni didn't know anything. She was being set up. She was innocent.

But her innocence was the least of Ethan's concerns at the moment. If he didn't get her out of here, she would cease to exist forever.

The map of the estate was a rough-drawn depiction, but it was better than nothing. Maddie had helped with the layout, and knowing that she cleaned many of the rooms, Roni felt comfortable trusting the girl to not get her lost in these warped halls.

Little Xs marked the vicinities where the guards stood, too numerous to count, a military entourage strategically placed, some spots more than others.

The two areas on the map that had an exorbitant amount of guards were her destinations. Whatever required that much muscle had to be significant enough to protect.

Like an exit.

Roni's bedroom displayed no clock. She could only guess the sun hadn't made its appearance yet, but it would soon. Then what?

She grabbed at the tail of her scarf in the vicinity of her pounding heart. She needed to keep her fear in check or she would lose her faculties. But physical torture was all too real to her. Years of pain from her burns and multiple surgeries left her with a need to be in the driver's seat at all times, never wanting to succumb to being in something's or someone else's grip again. The memory of being a slave to the pain of years of surgeries and recuperations with no end in sight and no reprieve nearly killed her. If it hadn't been for Cora she would have lost her mind.

Roni thought of the hopelessness in Maddie's eyes. That young girl knew the same merciless agony of having no control over her life, and no voice to speak out.

Roni pulled at her scarf harder, realizing her breathing had picked up to an erratic pace. In the mirror of the vanity, she could see her knuckles had whitened with their hold. The understanding that she had been brought to a place where her control was stolen from her again brought on a swift bout of panic. She had to get out of this place. Now.

But how, if she was under lock and key?

She looked at the map again. Thanks to Maddie, Roni wouldn't be walking blind when she did somehow get out of the room. The girl would be compensated for her help big-time. Roni told her that, but the girl shook her head back and forth. How strange that Maddie wouldn't hesitate to help another captive escape but refused help for herself. She didn't believe it yet, but when the time came to put this place in the rearview mirror, Maddie would be buckled in beside Roni.

But first to find a vehicle to make a break in.

There had to be a slew to choose from. What high-class criminal didn't brandish a showroom full of souped-up horsepower?

She looked at the area on the map with all the guards, the place the cars were kept. Every detail of the route would have to be memorized. She couldn't keep the map lying around. If it was confiscated, Maddie would pay the price. Flushing it was the only way to prevent fallout and to protect her new friend.

When she thought she had it imprinted on her brain, Roni made her way to the bathroom and watched it disappear. Oh, how she wished she could do the same. Press a button and poof, back in her own house on her mountain in Norcastle, safe from anyone who wanted to harm her. All she could do was be ready to run when the guards weren't watching.

A knock sounded on her door.

Could this be her opportunity? The lock clicked over, and Roni had one second to make her play.

She reached for a mosaic vase on the dresser and ran at the door. As it pushed wide into the room, she couldn't see who entered behind it. At full force she barreled at the door and slammed into it with her shoulder, her arm raised high over her head with the vase ready to find its target.

As she heaved her body at the door, she knocked her visitor into a stumble. It took her a second to realize it was Gunn and less than another second to bring the vase down.

But before she could make contact, he turned his body, his arm reaching up to block her assault. He grabbed on to the vase. A battle of strength kept it high in the air, their face levels matched and close.

"Roni, I'm here to help you," he said, his eyes filled with the compassion he'd lacked back in the garage. Surely a trick.

And she wasn't falling for it. "My name is Veronica Spencer. Roni is for friends *only*."

Gunn pulled the vase from her hand with little effort and tossed it onto the bed. He grasped her wrist still above her head with his free hand. "Then Roni it is, because from where I stand, I'm the only friend you've got."

FOUR

"You're nothing but a criminal." Roni spoke low, less than an inch from Ethan's face. He could feel her rapid breathing brush his lips, the only sign of fear she emitted, and he would have missed it if he hadn't closed in to protect himself from her assault. Not that he blamed her. Why should she believe him to be anything but a criminal?

"I know what it looks like, but you need to trust me. I'm your friend."

"Friends don't kidnap you and put you in danger."

Ethan slowly released her wrist and stepped back toward the door, his hands raised to show he meant no harm. He pushed the door ajar, just enough to hear the manpower out looking for him coming. He peered through the crack, knowing it could be any second. He'd raced down here as soon as Ramsey and Guerra left the office to join the guards. "Are you sure about that? Because from what I just learned you're in this situation because one of your so-called friends put you here."

Roni came at him, her pointer finger raised to his chest. "I'm here because *you* put me here." Her ice-blue eyes crystallized as she went head-to-head with him.

The woman believed him to be dangerous, and yet, she didn't let that stop her from defending herself. He would hate to be on her blacklist. Something told him she would be relentless in her revenge tactics.

Perhaps it wasn't a friend after all who put her in this situation.

"How many enemies do you have, Roni Spencer? I'm going to need the list."

"The only thing you'll be getting from me is my dust. And a slammer in your face. And you can tell *your* so-called friends the same thing. You're all going down. Believe me when I tell you that you're going to wish you let Guerra kill me."

"Shall I call him upstairs?"

"You wouldn't dare."

"You're right, I wouldn't, but I need you to listen to me if I'm going to get you out of here and someplace safe."

"And why would I let you take me anywhere else after you already brought me to such a horrid place? Do you know there are people kept here against their will? I'm not the only one."

"Yes, I know, but right now my only concern is getting you out of here."

"Why?"

Because I'm a federal agent who got you into this place, and now I feel responsible.

Blowing his cover wasn't an option. There had to be another way to gain Roni's trust. But how, when honesty was the best policy for such a thing?

But honesty is what nearly got his last civilian killed when he allowed her to play a role in his work. The less Roni knew the better for her safety. Let her fear him if it kept her alive...and in line.

Ethan leaned in. "I'm in the business of stealing cars, not murder. I'm not about to go down for yours. I meant what I said before. Someone you know paid Guerra to kill you. Someone who feels you have wronged them in some way, enough to want you to pay with your life. If you want to live into your golden years, you better start trusting me with a list of all the people you have aggrieved in some way."

Roni tilted her head, her mouth still pursed in rebellion. "Would that be on or off the track?"

Great. Just what he thought. He wasn't looking at one list. He was looking at multiples.

Roni's ambivalent face in the three-way vanity mirrors proved her indecision from all sides. Her lips curled in distaste that she would even consider Gunn's offer to help her as legit.

She averted her gaze to the other face reflected behind her. To the man, himself, who should be paying for all the atrocities inflicted on her.

Not earning her trust.

His baby blues stared at her, waiting for her compliance. She searched for clues to any real innocence in them. An innocent criminal. *Yeah, right.* The idea was absurd. Insane. Crazier than racing without a pit crew.

Ah, and there was the clincher. She knew a racer was only as good as her crew. And she was as good as dead without a team to get her out of here alive.

But to trust a criminal?

"Clock's ticking, Roni." Gunn urged her to make up her mind. "If I didn't care about your life, I wouldn't have interrupted Guerra's handiwork at your garage."

"My school," she mumbled. Would her dream ever come true now? Would anyone but her care if it didn't? Definitely not Uncle Clay.

"What school?" the criminal asked.

Roni hesitated sharing anything with this man, but made the decision to test the waters. She'd find out soon enough if she dipped too far. She also hoped she'd uncover a little information about the identity of Gunn. "You can put Clay Spencer on the top of the list."

"Your uncle?" he replied quickly.

She folded her arms. "Interesting you should know that. Are you working with him? Did he give you and Guerra access to my track?"

"If I knew that I wouldn't be asking you for a list of your enemies. As for knowing he's your uncle, I like to check out the places we're setting up shop. Like who's running the joint and who might come after me."

"So that's how you knew I owned Spencer Speedway? You had me checked out?" Roni's hand went to her throat. "What else did you learn about me?"

"That's a topic for another day. Right now, I need to know why you think your uncle would want to harm you. Has he in the past?"

She hesitated. "No, but let's just say he's never been very supportive of me." She dropped her arm and moved to the edge of the bed, resting a hand on the bedpost. "For years I've wanted to open a racing school at the track, but he's stood in my way. Even tried to marry me off so I would walk away from the business."

"Marry you off?" Ethan huffed. "Who got the door prize at that bazaar?"

A laugh bubbled up Roni's throat and slipped out before she could stop it. She couldn't help herself, even if the joke was on her. "That is totally something I would say. You're a funny man, Gunn."

"Ethan."

She sobered. Too intimate. "We'll see, Gunn."

He gave her his striking profile as he peered down the hall. "That's fine. Back to the list. Who did your uncle want you to marry?" He faced her again, and she hated that she liked that view too.

"Jared Finlay."

"The racer?"

"Only because of me. I taught him everything he knows and sponsored him all the way."

"And?" Ethan asked.

"And what?"

"And should I add him to the list?"

Roni dropped her gaze to the floor, giving a reluctant half nod after a few moments, questioning how much more information to give Gunn. She would surely regret trusting him. Just as she regretted ever trusting Jared Finlay. Gunn should know how she worked, just in case he got any ideas.

Roni lifted her chin to the criminal before her. "You should know Jared's days of racing are over. No sponsor will touch him. I made sure of it."

"So you ruined him. Is that what you're saying?"

"I'm saying I know how to make people who cross me wish they never did. I'm trusting you as you asked. Don't make me regret it."

Voices drifted down the hall, followed by a deep voice bellowing, "Where's her guard?"

The Boss was back.

"Everyone was called to look for Gunn," someone else spoke quickly.

Ethan reached a hand out and twisted Roni's arm behind her, catching her off guard.

"What are you doing? Let me go!" she yelled.

"You think you're going to break out of here? Not on my watch." Ethan spoke so loud she ducked her rattling ear away.

The door pushed open wide, exposing the Boss and Guerra with more guards in suits. "What's going on? Why are you in here, Gunn?" Guerra bellowed.

"Caught her sneaking around the place. I was bringing her back to lock her up."

The Boss sent a scathing look her way, but it didn't even come close to the one she sent Ethan Gunn's way. If this was how he would repay her for trusting him, it would never happen again.

"See what I mean?" Guerra said to the Boss. "He's like a chameleon, but he always delivers."

The sleazy owner of this place turned his gaze onto Gunn. "You've bought yourself another day on this earth, Gunn. Miss Spencer, I'll expect you at my breakfast table, and you better have a good explanation for leaving this room. You can be sure there will be more guards posted, so you won't be walking away unnoticed again."

Roni yanked her arm from Ethan, but he sent her toward the bed with a slight shove. He made his way to the door before the men. As he stepped over the threshold, he looked back at her and caught her gaze. Something in his expression had her holding her tongue from spilling her side of the truth. Once again she wondered why she trusted Ethan Gunn. The man had just thrown her under the bus to save his own hide. He used her for his own gain just as Jared had. He should be receiving her wrath.

Instead, her lips stayed sealed.

Roni dropped to the bed for the first time since being tossed in here. The horror of what this meant floored her. Her panic tripled.

Why? What was it about Ethan Gunn that silenced her? He wasn't a killer, as he'd stated. She didn't fear for her life.

And yet, she did.

But somehow, it was different.

Her hand went to her neck and the silk of her scarf slipped through her fingers like water. One moment in her grasp, in her control, the next... gone.

She had her answer, and it scared her. She felt her control disappearing in the presence of Ethan Gunn. He had something Jared never had, even when Jared was in the driver's seat.

Ethan had power over her.

She never gave that to anyone. So why him?

FIVE

The long, red-carpeted hall leading to the dining room felt like a death march to Roni's sleep-deprived mind. Four guards now accompanied her. After Ethan portrayed her as the escapee, her entourage had been beefed up to maximum security. An opening for an escape looked bleaker than when she'd arrived. All because she'd been duped by Ethan Gunn.

Hello? Criminal. What did she expect? A man of his word? *Criminal, criminal, criminal*, she silently reminded herself, as she had done since the moment he had left her room a few hours ago. She hoped saying it enough times would release whatever hold he had on her.

It was probably another reason he came to her room. Yes, he needed to cover himself, but he most likely wanted to torment her with the hold he had over her.

Something told her he knew more about her than he let on. Roni felt her scarf's knot at her neck. A quick perusal, and she knew the silk covered her well. It would have to.

And not because of Ethan Gunn, she told herself.

The open double doors at the end of the hall were her curtain, and she needed to be more than the spectacle at the show. She needed to be the showstopper. Her life depended on it. And so did Maddie's.

Roni thought of the young woman. She hadn't seen the maid yet that morning, which surprised her...and concerned her. Had her owner penalized her in some way? Had he learned that she planned to help Roni escape? Had the man left Roni during the night for an impromptu interrogation of Maddie? Roni's stomach clenched at the thought of what his interrogations would consist of.

She passed a door with two guards posted on either side. Her recollection of Maddie's drawn map labeled it the door to the garage below. Getting through those men would take some figuring, *if* she could get away from her four, first. And who knew how many more awaited her below. Would she even get near a car to hot-wire it? She would need a diversion. The proverbial rabbit-in-the-hat trick. While the goons went all crazy for the rabbit on one side of the stage, she would pull a fast one on the other side. The faster the car the better, too, she thought, speculating about the models of cars below.

The doors were before her and her boots slowed on the carpet. The hand of one of her guards touched her back. Roni pulled away as though he burned more of her skin, but that movement also put her through the threshold into the ornate dining room on a rush. Her heels slid across the mosaic tiled flooring, glimmering like the surface of a lake in the setting sun. If only it could swallow her whole in this moment like one.

A raise of her eyes caught the dreaded man already seated in the head chair, his elbows resting on its golden arms in waiting. His tight lips said for a while.

"Sit," he instructed with a point for her to take the chair at the other end of the long table. An honor or a tactic? She would find out soon enough.

"Has my family been notified yet?" she asked when she pulled her seat in and mimicked his pose right down to his clasped hands at his chest.

He watched her but no reply came. The door behind her opened and a cart wheeled across the floor, coming up on her right.

Maddie stood behind it.

Roni jumped to her feet, scraping the legs of her chair on the floor. "There you are. I waited for you this morning. I thought maybe you—"

Roni cast a glance at the Boss, before finishing "—weren't well."

Maddie kept her head down as she lifted the serving dishes to place them on the table. She gave no inclination she even heard Roni. When she picked up Roni's goblet to pour her juice, Roni put out her hand to stop her.

"I can pour my own juice."

The liquid jostled over the rim of the glass.

"You were told to sit," the Boss spoke, his voice heavy with an unspoken threat.

Slowly, Roni pulled her hand back and found her seat again.

"You are not to address the help. They have a job to do, and it would do you well to watch carefully."

Roni picked up her napkin, opening it to fit over her lap. "Where I come from, we treat our help differently. Our maid is treated like family. She sits with us for meals."

"You will need to leave those notions behind. Servants are to be treated as servants, not family. Knowing their place is what makes them happy."

"I would have to disagree. There is nothing wrong with being a maid. It's a job to be proud of and blesses both parties. When they're paid well of course."

The Boss sipped his tea, and his eye twitched, accenting a tiny scar by his right eye. He brought the cup back to the saucer with a clatter.

Roni continued to speak over it, not letting it cut into her nerves. "My maid, Cora, has been with my family since before I was born. We're devoted to her as much as she is to us, and because of that, she's never wanted to leave."

Until recently anyway.

Roni kept that to herself. No need to go into the details of Cora's retirement. "All I'm saying is your servants might not feel the same way as you do about their place."

"Remove your scarf."

Roni jolted at the request. "I'm sorry, what?"

"You heard me. I don't repeat myself." Not a hair of the man's slick black hair moved.

Roni lifted a hand to her throat where the silk covered her scars. She quickly brought it down to grab her fork. "I would rather not. It's my signature piece. I'm never seen without it."

The scrambled eggs on her plate looked as if they would lodge in her throat if she dared put them down it. She reached for the juice and took a sip, then another and another. Returning it to the white-clothed table, she moved some more eggs around the plate. Her fork hit something hard.

Roni paused and looked back at the man across from her. Two of her remaining guards had stepped up beside him from out of nowhere. The Boss waved a finger and they moved down the sides of the table toward her, their eyes only on her scarf.

Roni wanted to move her eggs to find out what was under them, but she also needed to protect her neck from being exposed.

She reached for her napkin to blot her mouth and threw it over the eggs just as she stood up, upending her chair to the floor.

"Step away from me," she said with a glare at both men.

"They only follow orders from me, Miss Spencer. Something else you need to learn how to do, as well."

Just then Ethan and Guerra entered the dining room. They halted as one of the guards wrapped both arms around her, pinning her arms down so the other man could pull at the knot at her throat.

"Drop your hands!" Ethan shouted.

Roni willed him to look away. Why did he have to come in now? She wasn't ready for the disgust in his eyes when he saw what was beneath the silk. She wondered if she would ever be ready.

And yet, at the same time she wanted to shield his view, a hope blossomed that her scars wouldn't matter to him. What if he was different?

Before the idea took root, Ethan frowned.

Roni thought maybe the scars had already made an appearance, and he caught his first glimpse, but with the guard's hands at her neck, she knew that wasn't the case.

Ethan could only be frowning because he already knew.

After all, he'd checked her out.

Disappointment waged war with anger. Both responses were enough for her to fight her own battles, and she twisted with all her might to free herself from the guard's pawing hands.

Ethan reached for the other man still holding her.

But not fast enough.

It was over before she knew it. One moment her neck was covered, the next, her imperfections were exposed for all to see…and judge.

The man behind her dropped her as though she'd burned him. The one with her scarf held his hand frozen in midair. The Boss slowly stood, his hands gripping the edge of the table. She raised her gaze to his face and saw the familiar cringe, the distasteful curl of lips, but there was something different in his eyes that she was not used to seeing.

Anger.

Usually people's eyes widened and they looked away to some sudden interesting occurrence off in the distance. A child might stare and snicker or point and ask what happened, but adults never did. But they also never turned eyes so boiling on her that her skin could melt again.

"Kill her."

The words spilled from his lips in smooth clarity but bounced off her ears as her mind rejected the command as real.

Then the man who held her arms down before wrapped an arm around her throat.

Roni reached for his tightening forearm, knowing she couldn't stop the quick death coming her way. She closed her eyes, but suddenly the arm fell away lifeless in her hand. She had no time to understand why, but a quick turn of her head showed Ethan dropping the unconscious man to the floor.

He jerked his head to his left, and she took that as her cue to run for it, but a lift of his boot caught her attention. He reached for something and a tear of fabric could be heard.

The next second he dropped some plastic disk to the floor and stomped on it. She looked back over her shoulder and he shoved her to his right. "Run!" he shouted as he jumped up on the table to dive at the Boss who suddenly had a gun aimed at her. Roni fell to the ground. Her scarf lay in front of her, forgotten in the commotion of fists against flesh above her and around her. She grabbed the silk and pushed to her knees, her head peeking up above the line of the tabletop.

Above her plate of forgotten food and napkin, she saw Ethan had kicked the other guard in his dash across the table. The man now roused and gained his feet. He rushed at the back of Ethan, who fought the Boss and Guerra at the same time.

Three against one. He'd never make it out alive, which meant neither would she. Roni reached for one of the tureens of food and aimed it at the guard's head. It found its target and bounced off, eggs flying one way while his body went the other.

The eggs reminded her of her own uneaten ones—and of the object under them.

Roni reached for her napkin, scooping up the object in it. With no time to look, she fled for the kitchen door. It was time to get Maddie.

The door swung in on an empty kitchen. Maddie was nowhere in sight.

"The FBI is storming in right now." Ethan's voice halted her search. One look back and she saw Guerra and the Boss had him cornered. But his threat lingered among them all.

"You're a snitch?" Guerra growled.

"A federal agent, and you're both under arrest. This whole operation is going down today."

Ethan Gunn was a federal agent? The idea smacked Roni speechless. He wasn't a criminal?

"I should have known," the Boss said.

Guerra leaped at Ethan. "You're dead!"

Roni ran at Guerra's flying back without hesitation. Some unexplained decision in her mind pushed her across the room to help Ethan. With the full force of her body, she slammed into Guerra, sending him off his course. She dropped her napkin and scarf in the impact and landed hard on the floor in a skid across the tiles, the wind knocked from her lungs.

Her body jolted in pain, but her ears heard more than bones smacking stone tiles. They heard the tinkling of whatever was in the napkin.

Something black and silver skidded across the floor, stopping ten feet away.

A key fob.

And if she wasn't mistaken, the unique black crystal told her it belonged to a very special car. Maddie, Roni realized, had given her wheels out of here. And she couldn't have picked a better set.

On her knees, Roni raced across the floor and made a dive for the key—only to be stopped by the heavy stomp of the Boss's Italian leather loafers. But if he blocked her path, then what happened to Ethan?

Ethan plowed his fist into Franco Guerra's face. The punch felt liberating. He'd waited a whole year for such an occasion. Cuffing him would take the prize, though. And as soon as Pace got in here and threw him a pair of shackles he would do the honors. Until then, fists would have to subdue the man. Ethan took a punch to his solar plexus that bent him over. He used his hunched body to propel him into Franco's.

As the two went stumbling back into the wooden sideboard, glasses crashed in a tinkling cascade of destruction. Franco grabbed the front of Ethan's shirt and bent him back over the table's edge. He took a swing at Ethan's jaw, sending his head off to his right.

And bringing Roni into his view.

The sight of her stunned him, a response he tended to have since the first time he'd studied her picture in her case file. He had to admit, though, she was more than just a pretty face, but now was not the time to dissect those thoughts.

The Boss stood above Roni, a gun trained on that stunning face.

The fight with Franco would also have to wait. Getting to Roni before Lyle Ramsey's bullet found her took precedence.

Ethan lifted himself onto the sideboard in one jump. His legs tucked up and kicked out, sending Franco flying and landing on the long dining room table with momentum. The man's head collided with platters and smashed a vase before groans of pain monopolized his attention.

"Lyle Ramsey!" Ethan spoke loud and clear, choosing the most powerful words to stop the man from shooting.

They worked beautifully.

The Boss jerked his head to send Ethan a scathing look.

Ethan ignored it and stepped closer. "Yes, I know who you are. And so does every federal agent storming this atrocity as we speak. I'm sure by now they have everything they need on you to take you out of here in cuffs."

Ramsey turned the gun on Ethan—just as he'd hoped. Ethan didn't wait a beat, but swung to his right at the same time his left hand reached for Ramsey's inner gun arm. The gun went off, but Ethan expected that, as well. A step to his right before he reached for the weapon cleared him of the shot, and as his hand slammed into Ramsey's arm, the gun came loose and flew up right into Ethan's waiting right hand.

In less than a second, he had the gun turned on Ramsey and an elbow jammed up into the man's throat, bulldozing him straight back into the wall.

"Go, Roni!" Ethan yelled. He hoped she would follow his orders this time. At this point, Pace had to be inside. He would take Roni in, for sure, and Ethan flinched at the thought. He had wanted to be the one, to assure she was treated well until the record could be set straight about her. Pace tended to run a bit hotheaded.

But letting go of Ramsey was out of the question. He pinned the man to the wall. From the corners of his eyes he sought out Roni to make sure she listened to him this time and left the room.

He spotted her crawling across the floor, reaching for something.

"I said, go!" he yelled again.

This time she jumped to her feet and ran from the room into the hall, her scarf and whatever else she had been after in her hand.

No matter, she wouldn't get far. Whatever it

was would be confiscated as soon as Pace intercepted her.

Please, Pace, go easy on her. But would Ethan's word be enough to clear her? Guerra and Ramsey were sure to be tight-lipped. The only people who knew the truth were them and God, and Ethan knew God wouldn't be helping out either.

Ethan jammed his elbow harder into the man's neck. His lips curled as he leaned in and said, "If I were you I would spill everything you know about Roni Spencer and who set her up. It just might make things go a little smoother for you."

"Never," the man replied, his words gurgled in his closed throat.

Then he smiled the sickest smile Ethan had ever seen and Ethan didn't doubt his word.

Roni raced for the door that led down to the garage. The guards had hightailed it somewhere to save themselves. The coast was clear, but she couldn't go anywhere until she found Maddie. The girl had gone to great lengths to produce a car key for Roni to escape and wouldn't be left behind. It was almost as if the young woman knew Roni would come looking for her to free her. So why run and hide when freedom was being handed to you? The idea was ludicrous.

"FBI! Stop right there."

Roni paused with her hand on the doorknob

to her own freedom. One look at the man barreling down on her and she didn't get the warm
fuzzies. It was a tree trunk of a man, including
his thick neck leading up to a shaved head. His
hazel eyes glittered with determination, her as
the destination.

Ethan had mentioned something about someone setting her up to take the fall. This guy apparently didn't know.

"I'm not who you want. They're in the dining
room," she announced.

"I'll be the judge of that."

Roni pulled the door wide and let it slam behind her. She took the stairs two at a time and
reached the landing just as the door pulled open
above.

"Freeze or I will shoot!"

She didn't waste the time to check to see if he
held a gun on her, but took a right down a long
hall. Footsteps behind thudding down the stairs
pushed her into a faster run for the door at the
end of the hall. Would it be locked?

Roni reached it and sighed heavily when it
opened to a multibay garage. She turned the lock
and slammed it closed as the FBI man on her tail
hit the landing.

He shouted, "Veronica Spencer, you're under
arr—"

Roni whipped around and scanned the ten or

so cars before her. She held the key fob up and knew exactly what car it belonged to before she clicked the button to unlock it. The key fob was the most expensive car key ever made. Its dark shiny finish wasn't a finish at all, but sapphire crystals so the key never scratched.

She passed by five cars, all fast enough to hightail her out of here no problem. The Porsche would have felt right at home, but Maddie chose one even better.

Just ahead sat James Bond's most favorite car.

Roni's boots clicked speedily along the clean painted cement as her hand reached out for the door handle of the Aston Martin. But before she opened it, a movement inside stopped her.

Someone waited for her in the backseat.

Roni looked back at the exit, the door handle jangling from the FBI agent trying to break it from the other side. She looked back at the car's tinted windows. The known for the unknown.

She pulled the door wide, saying, "Who's in there?"

Slowly a face in the rear seat popped up. The black silky hair gave the answer away before Roni saw the face. "You—you said I could go with you, but if you changed your mind—"

"Maddie! No, of course not." Roni ran to the garage door and lifted it open. She jumped into the driver's seat and inserted the key fob into its place. She pushed it through and the car purred to life. "You're brilliant, Maddie, for coming down here and waiting. I thought I was going to have to go back inside to find you."

"You would have gone back in? For me?"

"I meant what I said. I'm getting you out of here. Now buckle up. We're about to fly."

Tires screeched over the cement as Roni floored the gas pedal and the car raced for the open door. Roni expected a blockade but wasn't complaining when her view stayed free and clear. She picked up speed and took the sharp right as if the car drove a straight line. So smooth, she reflected.

"You picked a great car, Ma—"

A man jumped in front of the speeding car, causing Roni to slam on the brakes, jackknifing it into a screeching side skid.

The vehicle halted inches from Ethan Gunn.

He banged on the window. "Open up!"

"Get out of my way," Roni replied.

"Roni, trust me."

"You said that before, and all you did was cover yourself."

"I had to, or we'd both be dead."

"You could have told me you were FBI."

"No, I couldn't. I'm undercover. That comes with stipulations, one being secrecy."

"And let's not forget you think I'm a criminal," she shot back.

"I did. I don't anymore."

"Well, your FBI friends don't feel the same way."

"Let me take you in, and I will do everything I can to clear your name."

"Get out of my way."

Suddenly a gunshot wrenched through the air, jolting the car.

Maddie screamed in the backseat and hunched down. Roni ducked as well, searching the surroundings for the source.

"Roni, let me in!" Ethan crouched low.

Roni clicked the lock over. Ethan opened the door just enough to jump in, and she took off before he had it closed. She pushed the car to reach its highest speed, climbing up into the hundreds with ease. The long stretch of road in the secluded area gave her a wide range and soon the digital numbers read 160.

"Roni!" Maddie screamed from the backseat.

"Not to worry, Maddie. I do this for a living."

Ethan gripped his own seat, his head plastered back to his headrest. "I've been undercover for a long time, but only now am I fearing for my life."

"Your choice, Gunn. Shall I pull over so you can get out?"

"I'm supposed to bring you in."

"Let's get something straight right now." She took her eyes off the road long enough to make her point clear. "You are only along for the ride."

He didn't seem pleased with that stipulation, but his next words were calmer. "Where are we going?"

"To find out who set me up."

Ethan looked in his side mirror, indecision on his tight face. "Neither Ramsey nor the FBI are going to just let you go."

"I've already gone," she stated, but neither of them missed the bouncing headlights gaining on them. The unasked question lingered in the sleek leather cabin.

Which of her pursuers would be the lesser of two evils? Ramsey, who had his operation infiltrated? Or the FBI, who always get their man and wouldn't take too kindly to being bested today?

SIX

A sidekick.

Ethan bit down on the backs of his teeth, disgruntled at being reduced to Roni Spencer's sidekick, a passenger along for the ride.

The tables had turned on him faster than her spinout back at Ramsey's. The woman could have killed him.

But she didn't.

The racing princess handled this luxury piece of speed with the ease of a bicycle. He shouldn't be surprised; he'd read her file. He knew everything about her life at the racetrack and her home life. How she'd lost her parents and baby brother to a car fire when she was three that, up until this year, had been deemed an accident. Recent events had proved the family members had been murdered when an order for a hit on the parents caused them to careen off the side of a mountain to their deaths. The whole family should have died, but two of the children survived, left orphaned and…scarred.

Roni's burn scars matched the ones in her file. He'd studied them on film numerous times, disgusted, not at her, but at the felon doing time who caused them. Ethan would have liked to hunt him down and make him pay with a lot more than time.

"I'll put my scarf back on as soon as I lose our tail."

Ethan jerked in his seat, realizing he'd been staring, and judging by the pain in his jaw, he'd been doing so with a look of distaste. He forced himself to relax. "It's not what you think."

"Isn't it? I know they're ugly. But I'm used to them, and you're not. I get it. You did well back in the dining room to hide your shock and repulsion. Better than Ramsey, that's for sure. I keep them covered so people can be relaxed around me and not have to find something else in the room to stare at. Or, in Ramsey's case, realize I'm really not the pretty girl he thinks me to be and decide I'm too ugly to live."

Ethan sputtered. "Ugly."

Roni wagged a long finger at him before retaking the wheel. "Don't even go there. I'd have to call you out as a liar. And then I'd have to dump you on the side of road like I did the last guy who lied about them."

"Finlay," Ethan said, but he wasn't expecting a confirmation. "The guy must be blind."

"Oh, no. His eyes were so keen, he could spot a scar across the room. He was forever righting my scarves. I know it was for appearances' sake, so I should be thankful, but still."

Ethan held in a laugh. She must be joking. "Thankful? Why?"

Roni shot a look of incredulity his way. "You've obviously been living undercover for too long. Out here in the real world people judge. It's hard finding your place in the world when there's always someone better, faster, prettier... not a woman," she finished under her breath.

The car sped along in silence. Ethan kept his eyes glued to his side mirror. More cars still piled in way behind them but couldn't catch up. Roni drove at such a high speed with the elegant ease of a queen on her throne.

"Excuse me for saying, but I don't think I've ever seen a better, *prettier*, woman driver as skilled and as fast as you."

A giggle erupted from the backseat.

Ethan whipped around, his gun lifted to shoot the intruder. He drew back at the sight of the black-haired maid from the night before. "You brought your maid? Are you crazy?"

"Some have said so. And I wasn't about to leave her back there."

"The Feds are there now. They would have taken her to a safe house."

"Right. Like they were going to do for me? Hardly. I saw one of your Feds. He looked straight at me and was ready to shoot to kill."

Ethan faced forward, resettling the gun to his lap. He tunneled a hand through his hair in frustration. "Pace." The man was as hard as granite. Working this job your whole adult life left a mark, but add the fact they had come from the rough neighborhoods of South LA and there was only so much turmoil a person could handle before the world hardened them.

Ethan looked at the flashy woman beside him. She had been through a hard life with the loss of her parents, but she wouldn't understand the pain of poverty he and Pace had grown up in. The set of her jaw as she gripped the wheel with strength and ability told him her stone could be just as hard as Pace's, though. Just as hard as his. But he had to think all that bling was just for show. She was still the spoiled little rich girl he'd read about in her files. She didn't know the pain of poverty.

"Pace is going to catch you, you know. I've known him my whole life. He won't sleep until he's got his man. Or woman."

"And I won't sleep until I've got mine." And with that, the car picked up more speed. The world whizzed by in a blur, sending his pulse through the roof. With his heart in his throat, he chanced a glance Roni's way.

The woman actually shined. And it had nothing to do with her bling.

Ethan had to wonder if he was wrong about the racing princess. He'd heard the tales of a few people who had lived through the pressures of pain but didn't just harden into stone. They came out the other side a one-of-a-kind diamond.

Did Roni know her shine was the real thing?

And what did guarding a precious jewel mean for him? A princess deserved high detail. He was a nobody from South LA. A genuine pauper turned cop. He worked alone for a reason. Nobody would miss him.

But if he failed at this mission, everyone would miss the princess.

Roni spun the steering wheel to the right to escape the sight of cars and SUVs in her rearview mirror. Her throat tightened with trepidation waiting to see if they saw her make the turn. Black cars appeared around the corner behind her and she had her answer.

They hadn't given up their chase. Not that she expected them to. She would have to lose them with something other than speed.

Straight ahead the road led to a main street four-way intersection of a small village. Signs

for the interstate signified another right turn and
Roni planned to take it, green light or no.

"Aren't you going to slow down?" Ethan asked
when she hadn't let up on the gas one bit. "You're
not making keeping you alive easy, you know."

"You just worry about yourself. And tighten
your buckle. You, too, Maddie." Roni gave the
instruction and reached for the emergency brake
with one hand. "Hang on."

The intersection approached and she could see
two cars waiting at their red lights in the opposite lanes. She hoped they would call the police
on her. But then she had to think Ramsey had
the police in his back pocket. How else could the
man conduct a criminal organization near this
sleepy little town?

"What do you think you're doing?" Ethan
yelled at the top of his voice. "You'll never make
that turn."

She turned the wheel, hit the clutch and yanked
the emergency brake in one move. As soon as she
felt her rear wheels lock up she released the brake
and hit the gas. The car made a perfect right angle
turn without flipping or crashing into the waiting cars at the light.

Or even slowing down.

The open road ahead revealed signs for the
interstate on-ramps. Another look in her mirror
showed a cluster of cars jammed in the intersection behind her.

She smiled. "Apparently none of your FBI cronies know how to drift their cars."

One look at Ethan's blanched face and dropped jaw said he had to agree he'd never seen anything like it. "You have to show me how you did that."

"You'll have to sign up for my racing school… if I ever get it opened."

"That was amazing. What could possibly stop you?"

"Who. My uncle is CEO still. My brother, Wade, left the business in his care when he left for the army. Uncle Clay has been against me opening a school since the first moment I mentioned it."

The blue highway signs drew closer. Cars whizzed by as she raced past them. The on-ramp beckoned on her right. The off-ramp faced the road on her left, but she only focused on the road that would take her out of this town.

Bad move.

"Roni! Watch out!"

Just before she could crank the wheel to the right, a small black Porsche screamed off the exit ramp and cut her off. It spun out to a stop, blocking her from the on-ramp.

At one hundred sixty miles an hour, Roni did the only thing she could do.

She took the off-ramp.

No other cars exited the highway at the moment, but that didn't mean one or more wouldn't hit their blinkers and take the ramp. Good, sensible drivers following the rules of the road, having no idea a speeding car with a woman racing to freedom would be driving straight at them.

She entered the highway facing the wrong way.

Car horns blared as she maneuvered between a few vehicles. They parted like a haphazard Red Sea.

"Another trick of yours?" Ethan asked, noticeable concern in his voice.

"No. I've never done this in my life. Start praying that I don't kill somebody."

"I'm not much of a praying man. You might want to do the praying."

"My prayers don't work."

A horn blared as another car drove closer, its sound warped as it flew past them and the speed of sound lessened.

"All prayers are heard by God," Maddie spoke from the backseat, her voice strong but filled with fear. "I never stopped believing that. I couldn't."

Roni and Ethan looked at each other for a brief moment, knowing how Maddie's prayers kept her hope of freedom alive.

Roni couldn't claim that Maddie's prayers didn't work. After all, here they were rescuing her from a place she never would have broken free from on her own.

Had God used this situation to answer Maddie's prayers? Would He free her only to allow her to be killed on this highway now?

And what about Roni's abduction? Had God used that situation to bring to light the people in Roni's life who were out to hurt her?

As soon as the road cleared, Roni yanked the wheel left and hit the clutch again to make the tightest U-turn ever. But when the same exit ramp neared down the road, she hit her blinker and took it.

"You're turning yourself in?" Ethan asked.

Roni snuck an absurd look his way. "No way. I'm going after my car."

Ethan shot a look forward. "That was *your* Porsche?"

"With someone else behind the wheel."

"Someone who doesn't care if you disappear forever. Do not approach that car, Roni!"

She kept driving.

"I know you heard me."

"But you apparently didn't hear me. I told you when I let you into this car that you were only along for the ride."

Unfortunately when she reached the bottom of the ramp her Porsche was nowhere to be found.

But the screaming cars of her pursuers were headed her way.

Roni hit the gas to race across the street and headed back up the on-ramp. The open highway welcomed her speed and she had the speedometer numbers climbing back to their 160-mph pace with ease.

Trees blurred by as Roni swerved around cars to get ahead, but she knew she'd have to do more than speed to lose the FBI and Ramsey.

"Do you think it was your uncle behind the wheel?" Ethan asked.

Roni laughed at the thought. But something told her there would be no laughing when she found out who it really was behind it all, not just the wheel.

"Someone with professional racing skills cut me off. Someone who knew my moves and how to replicate them. No, it wasn't my uncle."

Roni reached for her neck. She was totally exposed. *What would you think of that, Jared?* Would her ex-fiancé cover her up? Would he look away in disgust?

She peered down the stretch of asphalt for her car and gripped the wheel tight with determination of tracking it down.

There was only one way to find out what Jared would do when he saw her. But first she had to catch him.

SEVEN

Ethan gripped his seat as the Aston Martin careened down the highway at an unbelievable speed. A look in the mirror showed they no longer had his team on their tail. Perhaps Roni Spencer would break away from Pace and his men after all. That would really irk the agent in charge. How would the man take out his vengeance? Most likely make sure Roni never saw the light of day again. No amount of convincing the man that Roni was set up would work, especially without Ramsey's cooperation. And that man wasn't giving it. He, too, had a vendetta now.

"I don't think chasing your Porsche down is the best choice. It could be one of Ramsey's men with orders to kill."

"It's not."

"How can you be so sure?"

"I recognized something."

"You saw the driver's face? How? You were going a buck fifty."

"One sixty, and I didn't see his face."

"His?"

"Yes, his. Jared Finlay."

"Your ex? How do you know it's him and not one of Guerra's muscle?"

"I recognized the way he cut me off. He drifted."

"So?"

"So, it was perfect. Just like my turn back at the intersection. Just like the way I taught him."

"You taught him?"

"Everything he knows, not that he'll ever admit that to anyone. He wanted that little detail kept secret. He didn't think he would be taken seriously as a driver if people knew a girl taught him to race."

"You know what this means, right? The fact that he knew how to find you?"

"Yes, I know what this means. I'm not a ditz, contrary to what you might think."

Ethan pressed his lips. He couldn't really negate her words. He had believed her to be more bling than brains. "So then you must know chasing him down is dangerous. He wanted you dead, Roni. He didn't care what Guerra did with you or where you ended up. You don't know this, but Ramsey planned to export you like inventory. These aren't people you can just walk up to to set things straight. If Finlay is working with them, then you're putting your life in danger by tracking him down. Are you listening to me? Roni!"

A sound overhead vied for her attention.

"What is that?" Roni peered over her steering wheel and looked to the skies.

Ethan leaned forward and, at the sight of a helicopter swooping in over them, he hit the radio button and scanned the stations until he found a breaking newsflash.

...pursuit on US Route 3. We're told Veronica Spencer is at the wheel and fleeing from the FBI. She's kidnapped a maid from the house as well as a federal agent. Spencer is wanted for grand theft auto and car cloning. She is suspected to be involved in trafficking humans into and through the country.

Ethan hit the button to silence the radio. He banged the dashboard. "You've got to be kidding me. What is Pace thinking involving the media?"

"Media?" She squinted up. "That's a news chopper?" Her hand flew to her neck, then patted around the front of the car until she connected with her scarf, lying in a silky heap. "Quick, tie this around my neck. Make sure nothing is showing." She held the pink scarf in his direction, a little shake to urge him to follow her orders. Orders that made absolutely no sense.

"You really are crazy. Your scars are the least of your concerns right now. You are being hunted down by the FBI, and they are using every connection they have to apprehend you."

She shook her scarf again. "Just put it on.

Please." She looked his way for a brief second, but it was long enough for him to see something he hadn't seen in her eyes yet. Not even when she was kidnapped and stuffed into the back of a van.

Fear.

Ethan took the material and wrapped one end around her neck while she drove face forward. He brought the ends together into a knot, his hand brushing against her mutilated skin. He paused when his knuckles made contact. Slowly he extended his fingers to touch her with the more sensitive pads of his fingertips.

"Don't." She took her eyes off the road and gave him a warning glare. All glimpses of her fear vanished. Or maybe it wasn't fear he saw in the first place, but something more defensive. Was her scarf some sort of shield to cover up more than her scars?

"No one touches my scars," she warned.

"Ever?"

She looked ahead and bit her lips. The helicopter closed in over them. "Only Cora. She had to since she was the only one to take care of me."

"What about your uncle?"

She huffed. "Never. Too squeamish."

"And Jared? You were engaged to him. He had to have—"

"Nope. Only to make sure I was covered at all times." She looked to the sky. "So hurry up before their cameras catch a glimpse of me."

Ethan nodded. "You want to be covered up in case the cameras are on you? What's wrong with people knowing you're scarred?"

"And here I thought you were smart."

"Just listen for a second. Perhaps a little glimpse could help you in your case. Paint you as the victim."

"I am not a victim."

He raised a hand to hold her off. "I'm not saying you are. In fact, just in the little time we've spent together, I can see you're a take-charge kind of gal. You don't roll over for anyone. Well, except for Jared."

"Not except for Jared. I dumped him, remember?"

"Before or after he covered you up like some sort of circus spectacle too grotesque for the world to see?"

"Thanks a lot. I'm not some two-headed bear dressed in a tutu. He knew the public wouldn't be able to handle my scars."

"Your scars? Or perhaps the idea of him dating someone with your scars."

"What do you want from me?"

"I want you to leave the scarf off. Not because it might help your cause, but because there's nothing grotesque about you. You're stunning and braver than any agent I've ever met. Hold that beautiful head of yours high and let them take all the pictures they want."

Roni hit the brakes, downshifting to bring the car to the breakdown lane.

"Get out," she instructed. "I don't know what game you're playing, but I'm not playing along."

"I'm not playing a game. I just want to help you. I know you've been set up, but my word isn't going to be enough against the mountain of evidence the FBI has on you. Let the public see you as the one taking the fall, not the one committing the crimes."

"Then all the more reason for you to get out. They think I've kidnapped you. Letting you go will show them that's not the case. You can tell them you got in the car willingly. In fact, you were being shot at by Ramsey's men and I saved you."

"Pace won't care. He will still take you down, and I will be there when he does."

"You enjoy watching ladies get cuffed and stuffed?"

"Only when they're guilty. And you are not." He looked out at the back window, catching a glimpse of Maddie also rubbernecking. "They're coming. What's your choice?"

She fixed her scarf, feeling her skin to find no scars breached the fabric.

"I wish you wouldn't do that."

"We do this my way, or not at all. Are you in or are you out?"

"I'm in. I don't like it, but I'm in. Now drive."

The car roared to life, screaming back out onto the highway in a blink of an eye.

"We need to find cover from the helicopter," Ethan said.

She peered his way as she took the next exit. "It's a good thing I know a lot about finding cover. To the trees."

Roni chose roads with heavy overgrowth of pines in the hopes the pilot of the chopper would lose sight of them. The whomping sound of the blades told her she still had a tail, no matter what she did. As beautiful and fast as the Aston was, Roni didn't know this car. Perhaps she couldn't pull away from them because of a tracking device installed in the vehicle selling her out. But that would mean only the car's owner could track her.

Unless Ramsey sold out to the FBI.

"How persuasive is this guy Pace you work for?" she asked.

"Very. Why, you hiding something?"

"No. Just wondering if he was able to capture Ramsey, would he convince him to offer up information, like how to track this car."

"That I doubt. I think Pace has met his match with Ramsey. I did my best to convince him back there to offer up the truth about you. Not even the threat of death worked. He just laughed. I had to leave him behind when I heard Pace give orders to go after you."

Roni nearly screeched the car to a halt. "Are you telling me you had that sick man in your clutches but chose to come after me, like *I* was the criminal?"

"Not *after* you. To *protect* you." He reached up to hold on to the door frame in the next sharp turn she took. "You have to understand how relentless Pace is, but I think sometimes he's too close to see the truth."

She checked her mirrors, looking for the ambush at any second. "Go on."

Ethan sighed. "We grew up together in a tough neighborhood. Well, I grew up following him around is more like it. He's five years older than me. It was a rough place, but he always looked out for me.

"Pace's sister raised him when their mother took off, but his sister wasn't much older than he was. When he was sixteen her body was found in an alley and everything changed after that. Pace went crazy. Not insane crazy, but determined crazy. Driven to get out of the neighborhood and clean up the streets. And to get me out, too."

Ethan looked behind him at Maddie. "Believe me when I tell you he would die trying to get you out from your traffickers." To Roni he said, "He would die trying to take down anyone he even thought was trafficking."

"And since he's not dead yet, he has always

gotten his man," she stated to show she got his point. "Pace won't stop until I am in his custody."

"Or dead."

She swallowed hard and missed her next turn.

"That's why I dropped Ramsey and went after you."

They drove in silence; the only sound was the helicopter somewhere beyond the covering of tree growth. At least it sounded a bit farther off in the distance. She could only think they were struggling to catch glimpses of the roof of the car and hoped that meant no tracker.

She came to a fork and saw a sign for a town ten miles away if she took the right.

She took it.

"This road looks less covered. Why did you get off the secluded roads?" Ethan asked.

"There's a town up ahead. Towns mean people and people mean phones."

"Who are you calling?"

"Cora. I need to tell her I'm all right. We have a safe room in the house and she needs to get in it. Something tells me your man Pace will use whatever or whomever to get to me."

"Why would he use your maid? Don't you think he would use your uncle first? He's family."

"Shows what you know. Your FBI file on me may list the facts of my life, but not the truth. Cora is more than a maid. She's the only mother I've had since I was three. Cora and my brother

Wade are the only family I care about. My uncle is nothing to me. And he feels pretty much the same way about me."

"Enough to have you killed?"

Roni held her tongue for a moment. She had secrets about her family that most likely never graced Ethan's FBI files. But people's lives were at stake—*her* life was at stake. And if her uncle was the cause, she wouldn't be held responsible for breaking her vow of silence.

"This is between you and me only. This doesn't go back to your leader. Got it?"

Ethan gave a tight nod.

"When I said I had family in the CIA, I meant it. Twenty-eight years ago when the car my father was driving went over the cliff outside our home, it sent us all either to our deaths or...wishing we were dead," she swallowed hard as she spoke, "but it was no accident."

"I know, I read the reports. Including the latest ones."

"But you haven't read the real ones. The ones on file were altered to protect those of us who survived."

"Your brother and you."

She peered his way and pushed out the rest. "And possibly my younger brother."

Ethan squinted in confusion. "Your younger brother was reported dead."

"Fabricated. His remains were not found in the

car with my parents. They weren't found anywhere near the car or the surrounding area."

"Why would they be altered?"

"Because someone wanted us watched over and protected, and with Luke missing, he couldn't be. If word got out that he wasn't dead, he might be hunted down. The files stated he was dead to protect anyone from going after him."

"So what does your uncle have to do with this?"

"He was friends with the killer."

"Did Clay know his friend planned to have you all killed?"

"He says no."

"But you don't believe him." It wasn't a question, so Roni didn't bother to answer.

"It doesn't matter if I do or not. Wade does. He looks to Uncle Clay like I look to Cora. As a parent. And now that Wade has found Lacey and married her, he can come home and begin to heal. That's all I ever wanted for him. To be whole again. He has post-traumatic stress disorder."

"What about you? Have you allowed yourself to heal?"

"All I've done is heal. Over and over again. Every surgery would start the process all over again. And as you saw, the scars will never really go away."

"I don't mean physically. I mean emotionally."

"Nothing to worry about there. I was only

three. I don't even remember the accident, and I don't want to. I've seen how Wade struggles with his memories. He was eight and had to pull me out while I was covered in flames. That's a memory I don't want to remember. Besides, a memory only makes you disengage from the present. It makes you lose focus on what's in front of you."

She nodded for Ethan to look at what was far ahead of them on the open road.

Her Porsche had reappeared.

The car faced her from the other lane, cruising toward her at the same high speed she traveled. A game of chicken. Who would turn off first?

"Really, Jared?" she mumbled.

"How can you be sure it's him? The car's still too far away. You can't see anything behind the reflection of the windshield."

"We'll know in a moment."

"Before or after you crash into him?"

"When I see how he avoids hitting us. I taught him how to avoid cars spinning out of control on the track. Cars are always coming at you, and you need to know how to get out of the way."

"And you think he'll be the one to get out of the way first?"

"I'm hoping."

"You're pinning this on *hope*? Great. I can't believe this is how I'm going to die. I've survived gang fights, drive-bys, mob hits, and this is how it will all end?"

"Thanks for the vote of confidence. I know what I'm doing."

The two cars careened toward each other. Roni pushed the car to its max, the engine sound of the Aston Martin blended with the oncoming Porsche's. The strain grew louder as the cars approached head-on.

Roni twisted her grip over the wheel, her eyes on the front of the car. Nowhere else. A car goes where the driver's eyes go. If the wall is the focal point during a spin, it will be the wall the car finds. Eyes on the track equaled control of the car.

Roni's focal point lay dead center on the Porsche's black, red and gold emblem. Her focus so strong she barely heard the sound of another motor approaching.

"Roni!" Ethan yelled. "The helicopter's back!"

She ignored him.

She gripped the wheel harder, her head pushed forward as though it would propel her faster at her Porsche.

"Roni! The helicopter is barreling straight down at us. They have guns!"

For the first time ever in her driving experience, Roni took her eyes off the road. At the same moment, a flash of gunfire sprayed out from the long barrel of a huge gun aimed straight at her. She'd escaped whole races of cars spinning out of control and gunning for her, but never did she think she would need to be fast enough to escape actual bullets.

EIGHT

Ethan needed to take control of this situation. Now. Roni may think she was in charge and he was just along for the ride, but he didn't work that way. He worked alone, only. How could he forget that critical fact? Critical because depending on other people got you killed. Or worse. He got them killed.

"Take the right!" he shouted, reaching for the wheel. His hand covered Roni's and turned the wheel just as bullets blew out the rear passenger side window. The Porsche spun out in front of them and Maddie screamed from the back. If he hadn't turned the wheel the bullets would have come through their front windshield.

With no time to dwell on the outcome of that scenario, he yelled, "Maddie, get down on the floor! Roni, drive!"

Roni took the turnoff. She sped forward, but her face paled and gone was the bravado she'd held on to since her kidnapping. Good. About time things got real for her.

She shouted with a screech to her voice, "I can't outdrive guns! Especially not ones coming from helicopters! I thought they were news crews shooting film, not guns!"

"They call it organized crime for a reason. People are kept in back pockets, and we can't trust anyone."

"Including your boss! How do I know it's not him up there? How do *you* know it's not?"

The fact was, Ethan didn't. Pace always got his man, and would again, even if that meant he took his friend out in the process. If Pace believed her to be a kidnapper of a federal agent, he would shoot first.

Ethan regrouped. "I need a phone. I need to call him and tell him to stand down. I've got this under control."

"Meaning what?"

"Meaning I'm taking you in before they take you out. You're no longer in charge. I am. I can't get you out of this if we're running from the law. Get to the nearest phone, and I'll set up a meeting place."

Roni's lips trembled, but she frowned, her head shaking in defiance.

"Yes, Roni. It's for the best. This can't end any other way. You know it as well as I do."

"So I'm just supposed to turn myself in as if I've done something wrong?"

"We will get your name cleared. But as long as you're running, you look guilty."

"We? Who's we?"

"You and me. I know you've been set up. I don't have the evidence other than an overheard conversation, but I will uncover it. I promise."

She drove in fuming obedience, but Ethan took that as a good sign. She was seeing reason, and even if it made her mad, she would do the right thing.

At a road sign pointing left for gas and food, she turned. Ethan leaned back in his seat, his eyes glued to his passenger side mirror. The distant sound of the helicopter told him they were still out there. The overgrowth of trees allowed for cover, but all it would take was one glimpse of the rooftop through the new spring blooms on the branches, and the chopper's gunman would have his target back in his scope.

"You're doing the right thing, Roni."

"What if I'm tired of doing the right thing? The right thing is always for someone else's benefit, and I'm always the one putting on the face to cover up the sacrifice."

"You'll be sacrificing your life if you don't turn yourself in. They weren't shooting to blow out tires. They were shooting to kill. If that was one of Ramsey's men, you'll need the FBI for protection."

"And if it was the FBI, who will protect me then?"

"I will. I haven't let you out of my sight for a reason. No harm will come to you from my men as long as I still have breath in me. From anyone for that matter."

A gas station with a convenience store appeared down the road on the right. She reached it in record time and pulled the car around the back, wedging it between a tree and a Dumpster. The garbage bin acted as a wall of cover for the car.

"Maddie, stay down," Roni instructed while opening the door. She looked to both sides of the building before making a run for the back employee entrance. Ethan followed her in but stopped her before she made herself known to the worker at the counter. The young man, shirt-tails hanging out, drummed his fingers on the counter while a small television broadcasted into the empty store.

Ethan placed a finger on Roni's chin and turned her face to his. His finger then went to his lips. "Let me do the talking," he mouthed.

"Why?"

"Because I'm in charge now, remember?"

She made the symbol of a phone with her hand to her ear and mouthed back, "I want to make a phone call, too."

"No. Too risky. You'll make your phone call in custody." His voice rose to a whisper.

Her arms crossed at her front. "Why do I get the feeling my sacrifice is for your benefit?"

Ethan paused before stepping out. "Maybe it is, but it's not for my career, if that's what you're thinking. It's for my sanity, and for your life." He reached out for the biggest pair of sunglasses on the sunglasses swivel stand and placed them on her face.

"So now you're covering me up too?"

Ethan bored into the dark lenses; her words froze his hands on the arms of the glasses. He wished he could look into her eyes. "It's for your own protection."

"Where have I heard *that* before?" She twisted away, but Ethan sprung a hand out for her forearm.

"Look at the television." He nodded to the screen.

She didn't move a muscle, the stubborn woman. He shouldn't care that she misunderstood his reasons for the shades. He should only care that she came out of this day alive. But for some reason nothing else mattered in this moment.

He released her arm to point at the screen.

Roni begrudgingly looked up at what played out on the wall.

Her picture was front and center as the news

reporter relayed all the untruths about her that someone fed into the man's earpiece.

Roni's head immediately dropped down, her own way of shielding her face from view. Her hand went to her neck and she adjusted her scarf that didn't need adjusting. Not to him anyway. Her scars were showing, though, and they might give away her identity, so he didn't stop her, but he silently vowed to stop her the next time she did that, and he knew there would be a next time. She'd reached for her neck enough times for him to know it was a habit, but instilled by who, he wanted to know.

For now, he spoke aloud to the employee at the counter. "Excuse me, sir, would we be able to use your phone?"

The cashier startled, stepped back and pulled down one of his shirttails farther. He squirmed a bit before he found his voice. "I—I didn't even hear you come in."

"Sorry about that. We parked in the back and thought we could use that door." Ethan maneuvered his body to block the screen from the cashier's view. "May we use your phone?"

"Oh, um, it's not supposed to be for customers, but we don't have a pay phone anymore either, so I guess it would be fine." He reached for the handheld and passed it over the counter.

Ethan took it and dialed Pace's info line set up for them.

Roni stepped past him and asked, "Do you have a cell I could use? I need to call someone, too."

Ethan's line rang as the cashier handed his personal phone over to Roni without debate. Before Ethan could stop her, she dialed the phone and turned away from him.

"About time you called," Pace said. "I'm working on getting a trace. Hang on just forty more seconds, and I'll come pick you up. And your kidnapper, too."

"She's innocent," Ethan whispered into the phone.

"She standing right there, is she? I get it."

Ethan looked at the cashier squinting at him, and then the screen. Then Roni. Ethan attempted to listen to who she spoke to, especially when her voice rose to a cry.

Something was wrong.

"That woman is a piece of work, kidnapping a fed. Unreal." Pace spoke but Ethan barely heard him over Roni's rising panic.

"Where's Uncle Clay? What do you mean he's out of town? What are you doing staying at his house? Get back home where it's safe." Roni's voice cracked.

"Ten seconds," Pace announced. "And then she is mine."

"Someone is setting me up. You can't trust

anyone. I mean it. *Anyone!* People are shooting to kill."

"Five seconds," Pace spoke with a little too much glee in Ethan's estimation.

"I could have died!" Roni cried out.

"Two sec—"

Click.

Ethan pushed his thumb hard over the end call button.

Call over.

And most likely his job, too. But Ethan had to take Roni's words to heart.

You can't trust anyone.

Ethan never believed that would include Pace.

Roni bent her head low to avoid the store clerk's inquisitive eyes. She covered her mouth and said, "You need to get back home. It's safer there. Get into the safe room and lock yourself in. Trust no one. Do you understand me, Cora? No one."

Roni turned her head to find Ethan had stepped up behind her. Deep concern etched his brow. His hand came to rest on her shoulder, but when he moved from his spot, something pulled the clerk's attention. Over Ethan's shoulder, Roni saw a glimpse of his face on the television screen. She shot a look at the clerk in the same moment the young guy's eyes widened on Ethan. His head bounced between them as realization of who they were hit him dead center.

Slowly, the man moved up to the counter. Roni jerked her head for Ethan to take notice. Forget about concern for her phone call. Something else was about to go down right in front of them.

Roni dropped the phone on the counter. "Thank you for letting us use the phone."

The clerk nodded as his hand reached under the counter.

"I wouldn't do that if I were you," Ethan said.

"And why not?" The clerk stilled.

"Because I'm a federal agent, and it won't end well for you."

The clerk tossed his hair at the screen. "They say you've been kidnapped."

"Does it look like I'm being held against my will?"

The clerk looked back at Roni. She held up her hands to show she had no weapon.

The clerk stammered, "I—I suppose not. But—"

"But we are being hunted down and need your help."

"My help? I'm not giving you my gun, if that's what you're thinking. Since I've been employed here, I've been robbed three times. I got a permit to protect myself. And judging by what the news is saying about you, I need to protect myself from you two. They're saying there's a chance you've gone rogue, and to consider you dangerous. That she's kidnapped a young girl."

"Rescued," Roni said. "I rescued her from a man who bought her and kept her locked up. He also had me locked up. I was able to escape, but now I need to clear my name from someone who set me up."

"Why should I believe you?" A click came from below the counter.

A shuffling sound stole all their attentions. "Because it's true," a soft, timid voice spoke. "They didn't kidnap me. They freed me."

"Maddie!" Roni spun around. "You should have stayed in the car."

"The helicopter flew overhead. I thought they might come back. I thought they might shoot at the car again."

"I parked it as close to the woods as possible so it wouldn't be seen."

"I didn't want to stay. And I'm glad I didn't. Sir, please don't hurt these people. They helped me. They're so good. God sent them to me." Maddie came around Roni so fast, neither of them had time to stop her.

Both Ethan and Roni reached for Maddie to try to pull her back out of the line of fire, but Maddie dug in her heels and widened her arms out to stop them.

"Please help us get out of here. I can't go back there."

The clerk studied Maddie's pleading eyes. Contemplation covered his face as he sent glances to

Roni and Ethan, too. "You were really bought and kept locked up? Like a prisoner?"

"She was trafficked here," Ethan said.

"Trafficked? I thought that only happened in third world countries, or something. Not here."

"It happens everywhere."

The clerk looked back at Maddie. His eyes studied her and slowly he frowned and dropped his hands by his side. "I'm sorry that happened to you. I'll help you guys. What do you need? Food? Gas?"

"What's your name?" Ethan asked.

"Sam. I've lived in this town my whole life. I guess I had an idea that something illegal was going on at the big mansion. I just never thought..." Sam swallowed hard and looked at Maddie again. "I'm so sorry."

"Not your fault," Maddie assured.

"No, but I didn't have to look the other way."

The distant sound of the helicopter grew louder. Ethan raced to the front glass entrance. "They're coming back. As soon as they pass over, we need to make our move, in the other direction."

Sam came out from behind the counter. "Grab what you want off the shelf. I'll get a container from the back and fill it with gas for your car."

Sam reached over the counter. He withdrew a small .22 and handed it to Ethan. "It won't do much but slow someone down. It sounds like you're up against bigger guns than this."

Ethan reached down and removed his .45 Glock. "Keep it. I have my own."

Sam's face paled as he pocketed his smaller weapon. "You're right. It wouldn't have ended well for me."

Roni took Maddie's hand as the young woman said, "Thank you, Sam, I pray you will be safe from no more robberies."

"Wait. You're praying for me?"

"I will always pray for you. You helped me today."

"No one's ever prayed for me before," he mumbled in confusion. Roni understood the feeling. She knew Cora used to pray for her, but those days were long gone. Especially after she told her maid not to bother anymore. The prayers didn't work.

The helicopter overhead had them all rushing to get ready to make a run for it. As soon as the chopper passed on they could make their move.

Except, the sound of the rotating blades remained above them.

Ethan snuck to the edge of a window. He peered up through the glass. "They're hovering."

"They must know we're in here." Roni rushed up behind Ethan. He put his hand out to stop her from getting closer to the glass. "What are we going to do?"

As if her question was heard above, a voice came over a loudspeaker. "We know you're in the store. Come out with your hands up."

NINE

"'Let us throw off everything that hinders,'" Maddie spoke into the tension-filled convenience store. "'And let us run with perseverance the race marked out for us, fixing our eyes on Jesus.'"

Ethan took his attention away from surveying the scene outside. "What does that mean?" he asked.

"It's a promise from the Bible. Jesus has already gone before you. He has marked out your path. You can't stop now, but you must let go of the things that hinder you." Maddie put her hand on her chest. "Forget about me. Leave me here. I'm just going to slow you down."

"No!" Roni ran back to the girl, grabbing her upper arms. "I am not leaving you behind. What if Ramsey's men find you? Or if the authorities get to you first, they might deport you back to your family who sold you in the first place."

"My mother believed in the fairy tale that I

would be given a better life. I don't fault her for selling me."

"But can you go back?"

"No." Maddie dropped her gaze for a moment. "I can never go home. But I can't hold you back either. I'm hindering you just like the scripture says. Leave me here, and make a run for it. Please. I want you to be free. That's all I've wanted from the moment I met you."

"You believe in freedom for me, but not for you. Why? Why can't you see freedom is for both of us?"

"Believe it or not, Roni, I'm already free."

"I don't understand."

"I know you don't, but I pray someday you will."

Ethan watched the exchange between the women while he kept one eye to the sky. "You ladies forget I'm in charge now, and I'm not leaving anyone behind."

Maddie frowned. "You, too, Agent Ethan, have things hindering you that you have to let go of. Not only me. You can't win your race if you are tangled up in your past. You also can't win if I am holding you back."

"No," Roni jumped in. "Now's not the time to be breaking up our team. Now's the time we work together and become stronger. We need to stick together. You don't hinder us, Maddie. You help us. You swiped me the key to the car. I would have gone nowhere without that. And your exchange of the key to me was brilliant. As smooth as a perfect baton pass in a relay." She looked to the ceiling, insinuating the thrumming sound of the helicopter above. "This is just another exchange we need to make…but as a *team*."

"But I can't help you now. I don't have anything to offer to get us out of here safely."

Roni implored Ethan for his assistance in convincing Maddie to stick with them, a team as she called them. She didn't know what she was asking, the danger it would mean for them. He was supposed to work alone only. Nobody got hurt that way.

"Come on, Ethan. In a race, the runners only have twenty meters to make that pass. If they miss it, they're out. Disqualified. The whole team, Ethan, not just one person. The whole team. Our time is running out. Are you in or out?"

"No," Ethan snapped. "I am a federal agent. You are civilians. This is not a team, and I am in charge. Do you understand?"

Roni shrank back. She swallowed hard. "Sure. I understand." She pursed her lips. "So, what will you have us do, *boss*?"

Ethan ignored Roni's tone of degradation. She would have to learn his job was to keep her safe. "Keep away from the windows. I'm going out first. I'll wave to you to come when I know who we're dealing with."

"And what if it's Ramsey's men and not yours?"

"I'll stay under the canopy until I know."

"And then what? I follow you out and turn myself in? That's your big plan? I guess I'm not surprised. They're your real team. We're not."

"Just follow my orders, and no one gets hurt." He hoped. The last time someone got hurt his orders were also followed. A lot of good they did.

Ethan pushed the glass door wide and stepped out under the canopy. The helicopter's motor whomped louder as he left the protection of the convenience store. Still he remained under the canopy and clear from exposure. A few steps toward the edge of the awning would tell him who he was dealing with.

The smell of gasoline smacked hard, but not as hard as the realization of his fear. One peek out from under the awning and he could be riddled with holes. Not the best approach, but what else could he do? Call for backup, he supposed. But deep down he worried his backup was up above, already here and ready to take Roni in.

Or down.

Ethan took his first step out from under the canopy, but before he made himself known, a car screamed into the parking lot behind him. Ethan swung around to catch a quick glance at Roni's Porsche.

A man was at the wheel, but Ethan didn't get

a good look at his face because of the gun the driver pointed out the window.

Three shots wrenched the air, none at Ethan himself. Still, Ethan dropped to the concrete out of procedure. He lifted his gun to shoot, but two more shots blasted beneath the canopy.

Again, not at him.

To his left he saw the direction the gun aimed. Ethan wished he had been the target when he saw what the shooter shot at.

A propane tank on the side of the store.

Ethan scrambled to his feet and made it to the door at the same time he heard the car scream out of the parking lot. He ducked low, knowing what was coming his way. He launched himself into the store as a huge explosion threw him farther inside.

Glass sprayed in every direction as the women screamed and ran. His back stung from the flying shards. Ethan hit the tiled floor in a roll, glass slicing his forearms and palms when he pushed up to stay in motion and make tracks. Screams from the back of the store pulled him in that direction.

He had to get Roni and Maddie and the clerk out of here before this place blew miles up into the sky.

"Roni!" Ethan pushed past the pain his dive into the store had caused.

"Back here!" Sam called.

A quick glance over his shoulder at the blown-out storefront showed a crater where he had stood outside. Fire-extinguishing foam spewed down from the part of the canopy still erect, but the fire roared on. The whole station could blow when it found the gasoline.

Ethan ran to the back. Maddie's eyes were awash with fear as she glanced past Sam's shoulder. The boy had used his body as a shield for the women. Nice thought, but fire was a beast that wouldn't let a little flesh stand in its way.

"Get outside!" Ethan ran at them, driving them to move.

Sam snapped to, but when he stepped forward, Ethan caught his first sight of Roni—frozen against the wall.

Ethan reached for her. "Come on! We have to go. This place could blow if that fire isn't put out by the foam. Roni! Are you listening to me?"

Nothing.

She gave no inclination she even heard him. Her eyes were open. Her lashes blinked. Her hand held her neck.

Her hand held her neck.

The sight before Ethan nearly undid him. Suspended in her painful memories, he knew her mind sheltered her from more. Ethan reached his arms around her and scooped her up in a cradle hold. "I've got you. Do you hear me, Roni? I've got you. You're okay. You're safe."

Sam held the door for Ethan to make his escape. The car remained in its hiding place beneath the trees. The three of them ducked as they made their way to the car, but a quick glance overhead showed the helicopter was gone. His head craned to see where the enemy might be, but a second fire off to his right stopped his surveillance.

The helicopter lay crashed and burning.

But how?

Ethan pulled the passenger door wide and placed Roni gently there. He buckled her in as he realized when the explosion threw him into the store, it must have shot up and brought the helicopter down, as well.

Pace.

Ethan ran around to the driver's door but couldn't get in. Not until he knew if his lifelong friend was in that burning chopper.

"Sir?" Sam called from the backseat of the car. The boy's voice shook. "Shouldn't we get out of here? This whole place could blow up."

Ethan nodded to Sam but still didn't take his seat. His gaze wandered to Roni's ashen face.

Flames danced in the reflection of her glassy eyes. He followed her line of vision to the shooting billows. What was going through her mind? he wondered. The way she still grabbed her neck gave him a hint.

A pain that went beyond his pain of poverty.

He'd misjudged her on so many levels. Saying she wouldn't understand real pain had been a major slipup on his part. He wronged her, but he wouldn't do it again.

Ethan made his decision and took the driver's seat. He fitted the rectangular key into the ignition. The car purred to life and he put it in gear, passing the flaming helicopter without a glance. He didn't need to look for the driver of Roni's Porsche to know he was long gone. Did the guy know his foil had been foiled? Did he know he actually might have saved them all, instead?

Ethan looked over at Roni after he pulled out on the open road. Her head turned to watch the flames get smaller and smaller as he sped the car away from the site. He reached for her hand still on her neck, glad when she didn't fight him.

So cold her hand felt in his palm.

So lifeless, too. She may not have fought him when she let him take her hand, but she didn't offer anything either.

Ethan thought it strange that her coldness bothered him. He, himself, never gave anything to anyone either. The two of them were cut from the same cloth. Two Lone Rangers forging their own paths in life, alone but in charge.

But alone never felt so cold.

Uncle Clay was right. What was she thinking opening a racing school? She didn't have what it took, but it had nothing to do with being a woman in a man's sport.

"I'm not qualified," she mumbled, the first words since the explosion.

Ethan squeezed her hand. She looked down and noticed dried blood on his. The sight of blood never bothered her. Racers were always getting banged up and in need of bandaging. Roni had even bandaged her sister-in-law up one night when she had been shot. Roni never got squeamish.

But apparently she froze at being in a fire.

She'd seen them from afar on the racetrack, but had never been in one...except for the one as a child.

"What aren't you qualified for?" Ethan asked, his voice low and concerned.

"Opening a racing school."

"I've seen you drive. You're qualified."

Roni slowly turned her head in his direction, blinking to snap out of the shock of her limitations. Limitations she never knew she had. "I always thought so, too. I thought I could deliver. I taught Jared to race and brought him up the ranks. If I could do that with him, surely I had what it took. But what kind of teacher would I be if I can't be around fire? I froze back there. You saw it. You saw me!"

"Okay, yes, I did, but you can't make a life-altering decision in the wake of that scene back there. That was an attack on your life, not an accident."

"Accidents on the track can kill, too."

"Yes, but nobody wants them to. That's the difference. That explosion back there was purposely triggered, and the fear you're experiencing is because you were cornered in it with no way out."

Roni looked out the window, but the dense forests flew by in a blur. "No. The fear only came when the flames did. I've spent all my racing years learning ways to break away from careening out-of-control cars not because I wanted to win, but because smashed cars tend to catch on fire. I can't believe I never saw this before. I wasn't racing to the finish line. I was running for my life." Saying the words out loud raised her voice as more of her past actions became clear. "Do you know how twisted that is? Since I was three years old, I have tried to forget what caused my pain, but in some warped part of my brain, I played with the one thing I knew could cripple me again. It's as though I had to prove to myself that I would win this time."

"Is that why you took on Jared Finlay as a student? You feared him?"

"I didn't fear Jared." The comment took Roni out of her reflection. "What would make you say that? I ended that relationship with no problem, and I only entered into it as a favor to Cora."

"Why would your maid care who you dated?"

"She didn't, but she did ask me to teach him to race. Cora is Jared's aunt. He's her sister's son. Jared's father ran out on them years ago. He's a gambler and his addiction left them destitute. Cora asked me to teach Jared what I knew to help them. It was the least I could do. Cora has always been there for me."

"So when did you start dating?"

"That came later, when Jared started winning big. It was an exciting time, for both of us. He made a public profession of love to me. I thought it was so romantic. I know now it was a PR ploy to make sure the public thought I was only his girlfriend in the pits. Nothing more. He hated telling people I was his trainer."

"Sounds like a great guy. Made sure not only your scars were covered up, but also your brains. Was today the first day he tried to kill you? Or have there been other attempts?"

Roni faced Ethan, confused at his words.

"His method of choice back at the station tells me he knew you feared fire."

Roni looked to the rearview window. The station was long gone, but Maddie's and Sam's stunned faces in the backseat had to mirror her own.

"Are you telling me Jared caused that explosion?"

"I didn't get a good look at the face behind the gun, but it was a man and he was driving your Porsche. You seem to think it's Jared. So, tell me, does Jared have any reason to make sure you don't return home?"

A huge sigh escaped Roni's lips as she righted her scarf. A memory from the day she went to the media to set the record straight about their relationship came to mind, how Jared had been nothing without her. She'd returned home after to find a message tacked to her door. Or rather a picture. A car on fire.

She'd crumpled it immediately, hating the sick feeling the image caused deep down inside her. She'd tossed it, but the image would forever be etched in her mind. Even the model of the car. A 1980s Mercedes, black, four-door sedan. She owned lots of cars, most from her parents' collection from when they were alive, but she didn't own that one. Even still, the message felt personal.

Had it been a threat?

Roni thought of all the things she said to the press that day. She even went so far as to say no one should sponsor Jared Finlay. That he couldn't be trusted and would never give credit where credit was due.

She ruined him that day. Without her money

and with the lack of sponsors lining up to carry him further in the sport, he was finished.

"Well? Does Jared want you dead?" Ethan asked.

Roni swallowed hard. "It's possible. I killed his career by publicly burning him."

"And now it looks like he's out to burn you back. But this time, literally."

TEN

The headlights flashed over the welcome sign to Norcastle, New Hampshire. Ethan hit the blinker and took the exit off the highway. He wondered if he should wake up Roni and Maddie. But Roni hadn't slept in days, and he could probably say this was the best sleep Maddie had had in years. It wasn't long after Ethan had dropped Sam off at a populated location that they had dozed off. They must have both felt safe enough with him to do so. How wrong they were.

He should wake them up. In fact he should have dropped them off somewhere secure and continued this mission on his own.

The weight of his new responsibilities felt as heavy as the silence in the dimly lit car.

He had no business protecting anyone, and now, he had two women under his care. That's one more than the last time.

Solo or no-go. That was the plan, or get out of this line of work.

Ethan thought of his passenger in the seat beside him and of her talk of being part of a team. She made it sound doable, even desirable. Just like the woman doing the asking.

He glanced at her beautifully serene face relaxed in slumber. Air released from his lungs at the sight of her; he felt his body physically calm with her by his side. *How ridiculous,* he thought.

And dangerous.

It was solo or no-go in the women department for him as well as on the job. Things got messy when the enemy figured out your weak spot.

Ethan wasn't sure why, but he knew if someone wanted to get to him, hurting Roni would put him over the edge. His gut twisted at the image his mind created, and he couldn't negate the fact.

He'd turned his back on his job for this woman. If that didn't prove to him that she had the power to turn his head, nothing would.

And the enemy would know it, too.

All he'd done was made Roni more of a target. If someone wanted to get to him, they could succeed by harming her.

Pace came to mind as the first to try. The friendship would be cast aside for the job. His handler would be livid at losing his best undercover agent. He would be out for blood. Retaliation. That's how Pace operated. But he knew how to work the system to get it done legitimately.

Ethan knew there was no way he'd escape Pace's butcher block at the end of this. At this point, he would be of no help to Roni in that arena because he, too, would be in cuffs.

But then that was only if Pace was still alive.

Ethan thought of the smashed and flaming helicopter. His chest seized at the thought of his lifelong friend dead, all for doing his job—no matter how misguided about Roni he'd been, no matter how close he'd gotten to the trafficking case, Ethan didn't wish his friend dead.

Ethan blew out a deep breath with a shake of his head. He wouldn't let himself mourn his friend until he knew for sure that he had been in that helicopter. There was a very good chance that it had been Ramsey's men all along. But Ethan had to think if that was the case, then Jared Finlay may have actually saved his life.

Not that Ethan planned on shaking the man's hand for it. After all, Jared had only acted for his own gain of seeing Roni dead.

Still, if Ramsey's men were in the helicopter, then they would have surely blasted Ethan away when he stepped out from under the gas pump canopy. The Porsche's appearance right at the moment he was about to make himself known saved him.

Roni murmured softly beside him. Her sweet sleep talk so unlike her sarcastic tone during her waking hours made him involuntarily smile. He quickly shook the grin from his face when he realized the effect it had on him.

In response he squeezed the steering wheel tightly to strengthen his resolve, but then her head tilted in a way that brought her lovely face into full view. She smiled and he wondered if thoughts of him filled her mind as she had penetrated his. Thoughts of her safety. Of her beauty. Of her pain.

Of her relationship with Jared Finlay.

Ethan shouldn't care about the relationship between Roni and Jared—he shouldn't care at all—but telling himself that didn't halt the stir of anger churning at his core. The woman had done so much for Jared, given her all to lift him up. The man needed a few hard-knock lessons in gratitude—right after he did his time for falsifying documents to set Roni up. And let's not forget her kidnapping and attempted murder, too.

"If you grip that steering wheel any tighter you'll break it in two." The soft sweet voice was gone, and Ethan smiled even bigger in the darkened cabin. "A racer's first rule is to ease up on the wheel. A tight grip does not mean you're in control of the car."

Ethan glanced Roni's way to find her straightening up in the passenger seat. Her hands went to her neck and righted her scarf.

"Do you do that on purpose, or is it just automatic?"

"Do what?" She brought her hand down from her neck slowly.

"Never mind. Teach me some more racing tips. If I was to sign up for one of your courses, how would you teach me to control a car like this?"

"Well, first off, if you're in control, you're not going fast enough."

Ethan laughed out loud. "Oh, man, I think I'm in love." The flippant words lodged in his brain and echoed over and over. Nausea rolled through his gut and threatened to make an appearance. He waited, *willed* Roni to come back with one of her smart, sarcastic retorts that would put him in his place.

But none came.

Instead, she grew quiet and gazed out into the black night on the rural New Hampshire roads.

"I'm sorry, I shouldn't have said that," he said, looking her way.

She dropped her head back to the headrest and let it loll to face him. "I understand. It's an adrenaline thing. But trust me, it wears off. I thought I loved Jared too when he proved a worthy student. The fast life has a way of tricking you into believing in things that aren't really there. After the dust settles, the truth roars louder than any race car."

When she didn't elaborate, he changed the subject. "Are you sure we should be going back to your house? It's totally secluded up on the mountain, and there could be an ambush waiting for us."

"Then we'll be ready for them."

Ethan nodded and entered the downtown village of Norcastle. Old brick factory mills-turned-apartments and restaurants lined the river off to his right. The road to the Spencer Speedway shot off to the left, but it wasn't the road he had used to sneak on the property with Guerra for the past month. That back road they had used to bring in the stolen vans was more isolated and unused for the most part. No one saw them coming and going at all hours of the day and night, and Ethan never saw anyone else on the road either. It was as though no one knew about the pass, or they were the only ones to have the authorization for being there. Another reason why Pace believed Roni was involved. He thought she was the one giving the authorization.

Ethan asked, "Has Jared ever used the back entrance to the speedway?"

Roni shrugged. "Not that I know of. It's nowhere near the paddock and track. That's why the garage has gone unused there. There's also plenty of room to install a training track for a school. People would barely hear the motors. I'd thought…well, I'd thought it would work."

He watched disappointment flicker in her eyes. Gloom hedged in on her dream of opening a racing school. Something in him wanted to fix it, wanted the Roni Spencer he'd come to know back in the car. "Keep thinking it," he said. "Don't let what happened in the past determine the future."

Roni's lips smirked and she rolled her eyes. "Wow. You might want to stick with FBI-ing and save the platitudes for the greeting card companies."

He flashed a quick grin. There she was! "That bad?"

"Yeah, that bad." Her eyes twinkled in the dashboard lights.

"Just trying to help."

"You want to help? Tell me how to keep from freezing up in the face of fire. You kept your head on straight while I folded in like a cheap tent. You're afraid of nothing. How do you it?"

Ethan took a sharp turn to start the ascent up the mountain road to Roni's secluded home. "We're all afraid of something."

"And?"

"And don't let this strapping, rock-solid physique fool you." He winked with a smile. "Believe it or not, I've shaken in my boots too many times to count."

"Like when?"

Ethan blew out a breath in a whistle. "I almost lost a civilian once. I tagged her with a wire to help gather some information on a case." Ethan squeezed the wheel. "I wasn't shaking in my boots when that went down because I was knocked out unconscious, caught unaware. When I came to, she was taken and the wire left smashed on the ground. A message to me that I failed. I vowed never again would I put another civilian in that situation. If I can't do my job, then I have no business going under."

"What happened to her?"

"She lived, but no thanks to me."

Roni eyed him quizzically, her lips scrunched. "I don't see it. I have to think if you hadn't been KO'd she would have been fine. I've seen you work, and you would have protected her with your life."

Ethan shook his head. "I failed her. Period."

"You were blindsided. It happens to the best of us. Just when you think you've got this, a car appears on your right and takes you out." She smiled reassuringly. "Been there, trust me. So is that all you've got? Because you said yourself, you weren't shaking in your boots."

Ethan huffed. Figures this woman would find fault in his confession of guilt. "Not terrifying enough for you? Fine. The other time was just this week when Guerra put a gun to your head."

Her eyes widened for a brief second before

relaxing into more inquisitiveness. How would she squash this one? Ethan found himself filling with anticipation to see how her mind would work it out.

Slowly, her head began to shake back and forth. "Uh-uh. I was there, remember? I didn't see you shaking in your boots. In fact, it was you who suggested Guerra kidnap me."

"That's the trick to hiding your fear. Don't ever let yourself get backed into a corner. Your fear comes out real fast. Always make the first move, even when you're scared. *Especially* when you're scared. Be the one to step forward instead of back when someone is coming at you. It gives you the upper hand in the situation and throws the other person off."

"Are you telling me you were scared about me dying?"

He sputtered. "You have no idea."

"Why? What was I to you?"

"A civilian under my watch."

"I was a person of interest, a suspect in your investigation."

"You were and still are innocent until proven guilty."

"Not according to your handler."

She got him there. Ethan sighed in agreement. "Pace knows better, but he lost his sister to a violent crime at the hands of traffickers, and I think his focus is clouded."

"So clouded that he would take shots at me from a helicopter."

"I hope not."

"But it's possible."

Ethan turned the wheel sharply to make the winding road that wrapped around the mountainside. A steep falloff led to a gorge down below. "Yes. But I hope I'm wrong," he said.

"Because that would mean your friend is dead?"

Ethan frowned and gave a quick nod.

"I'm sorry. I'm not sorry that I got away from him, but I'm sorry you're stuck in the middle of this mess. I guess I haven't really given much thought to what you're risking by helping me. Do you think you'll be fired?"

"More like arrested, especially when I tell them you didn't kidnap me. I came of my own accord and helped you escape."

"You asked me numerous times to give myself up."

"But they will say I should have taken you into custody and brought you in."

"So why haven't you? I may talk big, but I'm pretty sure you would overpower me."

"Taking you in by force is not how I want this all going down. Besides, when I called Pace from the station, I just got a bad feeling that he may be keeping me in the dark about something. I hung up before they could trace the phone number.

Or, at least I thought I had, because soon after, the helicopter showed up. More reason to wonder how they tracked us down. I'm not wearing my tracker anymore. So how else would they have known we were inside?"

Roni patted the dashboard. "Perhaps our ride is giving us away. I have trackers in all of my cars. I wouldn't doubt Ramsey did, too."

"Then that would mean it was Ramsey's men in that helicopter taking shots at you."

"Or Ramsey cut a deal and told Pace how to track us down."

"I've considered the possibility. I didn't want to believe it, but I considered it." Ethan felt his blood shoot to the boiling point. He hit the gas in response to the possible grievance. "If Pace even cut a deal with that monster, I'll—"

"Can you slow down?"

Ethan hit the brake. "D-Did you, Roni Spencer, just ask *me* to slow down?"

"Yes, it's just on these narrow roads."

Ethan took in her concern. Then it clicked.

"I thought you didn't remember the accident."

"I don't, but I'm not up to reliving the trip down the gorge to bring back the memories."

Ethan resumed a safer speed with a nod. "Understandable. So…" He peeked into the rearview mirror to find Maddie still zonked out. "What are your plans for Maddie?"

Roni craned her neck to see the sleeping young

woman. Her fear of these roads evaporated into determination for the safety of her charge. "That'll be up to Maddie, what she wants for her life, but I will help her any way I can. It pains me to know there are so many more people out there in her situation. I wish I could take them all."

"And do what with them?"

Roni shrugged. "If nothing else, look them in the eye and tell them I see them. I see they are people. A person before anything else."

Ethan dropped his gaze to her scarf and wondered if what Roni wanted to offer was the exact thing she herself desired.

To be seen as a person before anything else.

Ethan reached for her scarf, but she shrank back. "Jared lied to you, Roni. On so many levels. The man is slime. If I ever…" He retook the wheel but turned her way to say, "Take back what he stole from you by taking that off. No one will be able to hurt you again when you do. Not Jared, not your uncle, not anyone."

She stared at him, her eyes glistening in the light. "You're wrong," she said quietly. "This is my shield to protect me from people who would hurt me when they see I'm not whole."

"No, it's a shackle, and nothing more."

The lights were on, but who would she find at home?

Roni opened the passenger door as she took

in the massive family home built by her parents nearly forty years ago, and now left to her alone. All ten thousand square feet and a mountain to put it on. She hoped she would find Cora inside, but did that mean her uncle would be here too?

"Wait," Ethan instructed. "Let me come on the other side before you get out."

"I can open my own door." Her words dripped with contempt. His comment about her scarf bit hard, and she wasn't up for his kind actions when his words didn't match up.

"Never said you couldn't, but I plan to make sure you are alive and well when this fiasco is over. Humor me. I don't know what I'd do if I let anything happen to you." Ethan opened his door and closed it on a quiet click.

Roni sat back, irritated that his words curbed her anger a bit. Knowing his past that ate at him explained his all-encompassing need to keep her alive, but the truth was when all this dust settled his life would go on fine without her.

She hoped she hadn't cost him his job. If she died now, it would all be for naught for him.

For this reason only, Roni stayed put while Ethan came around to the passenger side. She stirred Maddie awake and stepped out to wait for the young woman to exit after her.

When the girl didn't budge, Roni leaned down and said, "Come on, Maddie. You need to stay with us."

Maddie looked to the house behind Roni, her eyes wide and frightened.

"Why are you scared? Do you know something? Are we being ambushed?"

Maddie shook her head but still kept her attention on the house. "Your home. Is big."

Ethan put a hand on Roni's shoulder. Under his breath, he said, "You can't blame her. Your home *is* massive, and her only experience with estates like yours hasn't been kind to her."

To Maddie, Roni said, "I would never hurt you. You will always be safe here. I promise. This is your home now, for however long you want it to be."

Roni offered her hand, and after a few moments of indecision, Maddie took it until she was pulled from the car and enveloped in Roni's arms. Together they were ushered to the back entrance by Ethan's guiding hand.

He thought avoiding the front double doors was wise, in case they did have unwanted company. It was best to sneak in unnoticed until they knew they were safe.

But the moment Ethan opened the door to Cora's private entrance, the unmistakable sound of a gun sliding a bullet into the chamber came from inside the dark room. Before Roni could make a move, Ethan shoved her and Maddie down to the ground.

A man's grunt followed, then the sounds of

flesh meeting flesh as Ethan came to blows with the intruder. More grunts could be heard from inside. Glass shattered and something or someone hit a wall.

Maddie whimpered. She tucked her head into Roni's neck, her small features wet with tears of fright. The girl had just been promised safety, and if Roni couldn't deliver that to her here, she couldn't deliver it anywhere.

"This is my home. This ends now," she said.

Roni removed Maddie's tightened arms and crawled over the threshold. Cora's apartment stood in darkness, but the moonlit silhouettes of the two fighting men could be seen, arms entangled, a battle of equal strengths, neither gaining ground nor losing it.

Ethan had plowed forward before the intruder got the upper hand, but he still didn't have the advantage, and he wouldn't until he knew who he fought.

Roni had to think if Ethan thought his opponent was his boss, a part of him would hold back, out of respect or even a little fear of taking Pace down. But if Ethan knew for sure the man he fought was one of Ramsey's men, he would apprehend the man in seconds, not caring if he caused a little extra pain along the way. And if this was Jared?

Well, Roni wasn't sure if she wanted to be in the room in that scenario. Things would not end well for her ex, knowing how Ethan felt about the…*slime*? She thought she remembered that to be his description of the man.

Roni reached for the light switch she knew to be beside the window. One flick and the intruder would be revealed, but would the light shed the truth on who set her up in the first place? Did Ethan fight her enemy?

Roni stood up before she flipped the switch. If she was about to meet the person who attempted to take her down, she wouldn't be starting on her knees. She would take Ethan's advice and make the first step in. She would be the one in control right from the start and, like her fast cars, if she was under control, then she wasn't going fast enough.

With her mind and reflexes readied, Roni flipped the switch.

ELEVEN

Ethan curled his shoulder in and heaved forward just as lights illuminated around him. His opponent's head bent forward, taking the hit with resistance and pushing back. All Ethan could see was the top of a black-haired military cut. Not Pace with his shaved head. Holding back in this fight was over. If that meant this would be to the death, then that was what it would be.

Ethan twisted and used his arm to lift the man's head just enough smash his forehead into his opponent's nose.

Blood splattered everywhere. The man hollered out in pain, his grip on Ethan's arms slackened.

Ethan spearheaded forward, taking the inch in this fight. He lifted his arm and broke free of the hold at the same time he jammed his elbow in the man's solar plexus.

"Stop!" a woman shouted from somewhere, but Ethan only zeroed in on his next move and took it. However, his opponent had anticipated the move and instead of the guy groveling on his knees, Ethan found himself hunched over, taking a hit to the gut.

He rushed forward at full strength. The guy slammed against the wall so hard that Ethan reverberated with him.

"I said, stop! Right now! Both of you! Stop!" The woman's voice registered as belonging to Roni. Ethan stepped back from his opponent, though not sure why he felt the need to listen to her and not finish the man.

His opponent groaned and lifted his head, his eyes also trying to focus on their surroundings.

The two of them heaved with crashing adrenaline, both unsure of why they were stopping from killing each other.

Except, Ethan knew why he stopped.

Because it was Roni who begged him to.

Ethan looked at the man and thought maybe he was her ex-fiancé. He tried to remember the headshot of Jared Finlay he had in her file. This man didn't look like Jared, but still, something in him sickened at the thought of her harboring feelings for the man who used and abused her so badly. She may not see it as abuse, but abuse came in many forms, and any man who made her feel as though she had to cover herself up was someone who used his influence to keep her down. That was abuse in Ethan's book.

His fists curled. Didn't she see Jared wasn't the man for her? That she deserved someone who loved her completely, mind, body and soul. A whole person, just as she wanted to be viewed. Someone who saw her beauty and intelligence and wanted to show her off, not hide her away.

If this wasn't Jared, was there another man in her life? Were his intentions legit? A desire to protect her from another man's schemes to use her overcame Ethan.

"Who are you and what do you want with Roni?" Ethan said, his voice low.

The man sneered. "I could ask the same of you."

Ethan studied the man's face at his confusing words.

Blue eyes that sparked in the same icy hue as Roni's looked back at him.

This man was related to Roni.

Family.

Another headshot from her file resurfaced in his mind. A military man absent from her life.

Her brother, but blood didn't mean he was devoted to her. After all, he'd left her behind at eighteen.

"Did you set her up?" Ethan asked point-blank. "Are you the one who betrayed her trust by putting a hit on her?"

The man turned his head to look behind Ethan.

Anger flashed in the man's blue eyes, more lethal than when they had been fighting.

The next second the guy pushed Ethan away and reached an arm out. Before Ethan righted himself, the man had Roni in his arms. Ethan nearly pulled him off her, but quickly saw how Roni clung to the guy just as tight. No one would be strong enough to break that connection.

It appeared his file had more than one thing wrong. Roni wasn't guilty, and she was loved.

Ethan did what he never did.

He stepped back.

The next moment, Roni's hand shot out and grabbed his forearm. She disengaged from the guy and said, "Ethan, this is my brother Wade."

"I figured as much," Ethan said. "But you'll have to excuse me if I don't cross him off the list of suspects."

"Suspects?" Wade said. "For what?"

"One of her so-called loved ones set her up to take the fall for cloning cars at her track, then planned to make it look like she escaped to some country with no extradition to live on the lam, but really they hired someone to kill her. She was nearly shipped off like a piece of merchandise, never to be heard from again."

Wade searched his sister's face for what Ethan wasn't saying. Shipped out for a life of despair and darkness.

At her nod of confirmation, Wade's lips frowned

and twitched. He clenched his fists and shouted, "Promise, come!"

Before Wade finished, a golden retriever wearing a red service vest bounded into the room. Without direction, the dog plowed into Wade's fisted hands and put her paw on his thigh. Wade sunk his fingers into her fur, his lips pressed tight.

After a few minutes, Wade seemed to collect himself. Ethan wondered at the extreme differences Wade Spencer fluctuated between and remembered the man suffered from post-traumatic stress disorder. His dog helped him cope through his shakes.

"Where's the girl?" Wade asked, still fighting against his body. "The news said you kidnapped a girl."

Roni walked back to the door. She could be heard consoling Maddie. Then she pulled the reluctant young woman inside.

"This is Maddie. She was sold to Ramsey and has been his servant for three years. I wasn't leaving without her."

Roni lifted her head as if she had to defend her choice to her brother. Ethan thought it strange she felt that way. Did her brother control her every move?

"And I'm sure you didn't think your cause through. Like you might be arrested for kidnapping, or worse, trafficking. That's what they're saying about you, Roni!"

The dog, Promise, pushed harder into her master's hand, quickly bringing him back down.

"I know what they're saying about me, Wade. I've seen the news. It's all lies. And now I'm running for my life from people who want me to die so I can't reveal the truth about them."

"Who?"

"That's the problem. I don't know. But it's someone close to me. Someone I trust. I called Cora and told her to come back here. Is she here? She could be in danger if someone wants to hurt me."

"Yes, she's here, but who would want to hurt you?"

Ethan locked his eyes on Wade, and after a few beats the brother shrank back. Ethan crossed his arms with an unrelenting stare.

"You still think *I'm* the person who set her up?" Wade pointed at Roni. "I would never hurt her."

"Perhaps you have hurt her indirectly. Perhaps your absence has left her unprotected by people like your uncle and her ex-fiancé."

Wade turned to Roni. "You know I couldn't be here. You know what this place does to me."

"I know," Roni said. To Ethan she explained, "Wade's PTSD was caused by the accident when we were kids."

"Murder. It was murder, Roni, and you know it," Wade said.

"And I also know Uncle Clay knew the killer. Doesn't that concern you, Wade? Doesn't that make you wonder if you're wrong about him?"

"He was lied to and taken advantage of. He feels horrible about what happened. We've forgiven him of any wrongdoing. Haven't we?"

Roni dropped her gaze and gave no answer.

"Roni, answer me. Have you forgiven him for his past choices in friends?"

"Sure, but I haven't forgiven him for everything else. For every attempt to put me down, and for his unsupportiveness. He was supposed to be our guardian, but once you left for the army, Uncle Clay took over the business and never planned on relinquishing it."

"So you think Uncle Clay set you up for cloning cars so he could own the track? Do you know how absurd that sounds?"

"Not any more absurd than an uncle who treats me like a nuisance and tries to marry me off around every corner. Yes, I think it was a ploy to keep his CEO spot at the track. He pushed me to reconcile with Jared. Got real angry when I said no. He wanted me to marry Jared so he could stay on to run the place. And we both know how Uncle Clay encouraged you to stay away. I think for the same reason."

"That was different. I needed to be away. I couldn't function here. Clay understood."

"Right. And I didn't." Roni shook her head and walked to a closed door. She opened it and Ethan caught a glimpse of a wide-open kitchen with the largest island he'd ever seen. She paused to tell Maddie to come with her. To Wade, she said, "Uncle Clay has been driving a wedge between us for years, and you have been blind to it. You've put him on this pedestal as a father figure when he's not your father, but I *am* your sister. We're stronger together, and he knows it. If Uncle Clay can separate us, then he wins."

"You're wrong. He loves us, Roni. He wants us to have each other. In fact, he's been helping me search for Luke. Why would he help me find our brother if he wanted to separate us?"

"Appearances. But something I've learned along the way is appearances are lies. I appeared to be Jared's girlfriend, not his trainer. Lie. An enemy in our midst has been appearing to love me. Lie."

A white-haired man dressed in suit pants without the matching coat stepped up to the door. His crisp white dress shirt was open at the collar and the sleeves rolled to his elbows. Ethan recognized the man from his file.

Clay Spencer, acting CEO for Spencer Speedway.

"And you think it's me?" the uncle said. "You think I'm the enemy?"

Roni spun around in surprise. "What are you doing here?"

"Sweetheart, we're all here. Where else would we be? Our Veronica has been missing. We've gathered as a family to try to find you and for support."

"I called Cora's cell today. She said you were out of town."

"Yes, looking for you. She didn't want to give anything away in case the phones are tapped."

"Why was she at your house?"

Clay leaned in. "You would rather her stay in this big house and on this mountain alone? Come on, Roni, think."

Roni looked at Ethan. Conflict warred on her face. She didn't know what to think. She offered a reluctant shrug. "I suppose it would be safer for her to stay in town. But I'm back now. Is she here?"

"You'll find her in the safe room. When you pulled up, we didn't know it was you. We had the ladies lock themselves inside."

"Lacey's here? And she agreed to be locked up? That's so unlike her. I would have expected her to pick up a gun and greet me."

Wade huffed. "It took some convincing, but she went. She's pregnant."

Roni's mouth dropped. Tears sprang from the corners of her eyes. "Oh, Wade, you're having a baby?"

"I wasn't supposed to tell you yet. She wanted us to all be together to make the announcement. I would say act surprised when she tells you, but after your stance on appearances, just be happy for us."

"Of course I'm happy for you." Roni reached for Wade, and brother and sister held on to each other. Ethan had to think if Clay Spencer thought to break the bond between these two, the man would have an easier time breaking into Fort Knox.

Ethan studied the uncle from the corner of his eye. A full head of white hair, neatly combed, topped a robust, healthy man in his sixties. He looked on his niece and nephew with what appeared to be adoration.

But as Roni said, appearances could be lies.

Ethan needed cold hard facts. He needed information that would shine the truth on how Clay Spencer really felt toward his wards.

Was he the good and understanding man Wade saw? Was Clay Spencer's continued position as CEO a selfless act for his nephew's sake? Did he just understand Wade's injury of PTSD and want to help him by staying on at the track so his nephew could heal? Or did he understand his nephew's wound because he was there and saw the fiery car crash firsthand?

Roni said the man was only a friend to the killer of her parents, but that could have been just another one of the lies posing as an appearance.

* * *

Roni held Maddie's hand and led her to the plush sofa in the great room. At first, Maddie sat on the edge of the seat, stiff and upright.

"Come on, I know you want to kick back and relax," Roni said from where she had sunk into her favorite spot in the house. She tugged on the girl's hand to encourage her to relax here. "I want you to feel comfortable here, Maddie. I meant what I said. This is your home for however long you want it to be. I'm hoping you choose forever, but I don't want to be one of those pushy friends." She smiled at the girl and tugged again.

Slowly, Maddie pushed her herself back, and before long, a sweet sigh escaped her lips.

"See? What did I tell you? Comfy, huh?"

Maddie turned to face her, and Roni saw tears pool in her eyes. "It's all so beautiful. I've never seen such a wonderful place. You have hanging glass from your ceilings like the Boss's home, but his home was cold. Big and cold. Yours isn't cold."

Roni looked up at the crystal light fixtures as though it was the first time she'd ever really paid much attention to them. A funny thing for Maddie to notice.

"He's not your boss anymore, and he never will be again. His name is Lyle Ramsey, and he's nothing but a sick little man, undeserving of being anyone's boss. A person in charge has to earn that title. They can never force others to treat them as such."

"But he did."

"And he will pay dearly for it, Maddie." Ethan stepped into the room and the conversation.

Roni followed him with her gaze as he went to each closed blind and peeked out from the edge. Full darkness had descended, so she wasn't sure what he could be seeing. There was no moon to shine light on anything. It was also pretty dark in the house, too, so Roni could only make out shadowy features on his face from across the room.

"Do you think they're out there?" Roni asked.

"If not yet, they will be."

Maddie pushed closer to Roni, tucking her head into her shoulder. Roni rubbed her gently to soothe her fears.

"It'll take some work for them to break in. My mother had this place built to withstand an army. Or at least until all inhabitants could get into the safe room."

"I see that. I checked every square foot of the place and know we only got in because we were allowed to. Your brother was ready and waiting, and I will be, too." Ethan stepped up to the couch, checking the barrel of a different gun than his Glock.

"Did you get that from the safe?" she asked.

"It'll make a good spare, and yes, I took it from your collection. I'll make sure you get it back."

She shrugged. "Take what you need. I wouldn't even know how to use it."

His sharp gaze lifted off the gun and onto her. "Then come here." Ethan extended his hand for her to take.

His open palm hung before her like a hot coal.

Strange how a moment ago she had offered a hand to Maddie and scoffed at the girl's timidity in taking it. And now here she was shying away from what could only be a hand out to help her.

Slowly she pushed forward, but taking Ethan's hand wasn't necessary. "I can get up myself." She stood and held out her hand for the gun, but instead of giving it to her, he took her hand and pulled her close. In one move he twirled her around so her back came into contact with his chest, his arm holding her tight.

His warm breath hit her ear as he brought the gun up in front of her. A shiver raced through her that only multiplied when his deep voice spoke low, vibrating across her ear.

"Put your hands on the grip. Leave your finger off the trigger," he instructed.

She followed his direction, though she wasn't sure if anything came after the first step. Her own breathing sounded so loud in her head.

"Do you know which eye is your dominant eye?"

"Pardon?" she said, her voice rising a bit.

"Which of your eyes sees the true target? You

have one dominant eye and one that is off its mark. Sometimes you only get one shot. You don't want to miss."

"I understand."

"I figured you would. You're smart like that."

Roni couldn't stop her lips from bending. Something about the way Ethan complimented her touched her. Maybe it was because he sounded so sincere. Jared used to sound like that. He would tell her how smart she was and...

Roni let the smile slip from her face.

"...you have to understand the basics of how a handgun operates. With the exception of .22 ammunition, most, if not all, other handgun ammunition is called centerfire rounds..."

Jared had always admired her intelligence. But then she was helping him advance in his career. He would want to encourage her to share all, she realized. So he could take advantage of all she knew.

"...the primer is a small self-contained cap that is shock-sensitive. When you pull the trigger you strike it. It sends a small explosion into the casing and ignites the gunpowder inside the casing..."

Ethan was different, though. He had nothing to gain in telling her she was smart. She could offer him no skills to help him climb the ladder.

"...gunpowder burns and the chemical reaction causes gas expansion, which fires the bullet. Understand so far?"

She nodded, feeling the side of his cheek hit against her neck when she moved. "Sorry."

"For what?"

"I didn't mean to bump you with my neck."

His face so close to hers stilled. "Why would that bother me?"

"Because it's gross. Even with the scarf on."

He brought the gun down by his side and spun her around. His arm no longer engulfed her, and she missed it instantly.

Anger scorched her from deep within his eyes. "Take it off," he demanded.

Her hand went to her neck. "I already told you no."

"I thought you said you were done with appearances. Lady, you walk around every day flashing the brightest appearance of anyone."

Roni pressed in, undaunted. "You're right. I won't lie. It is an appearance. If people knew the truth—"

"They wouldn't care."

"You're wrong. You haven't lived with the looks of disgust that flash on people's faces before they can catch their reactions."

"Sweetheart, I know all about looks of disgust. I may not have physical scars, but being a dirty kid from the hood had the same effect. There was no covering that stench up. People could smell me from across the room. I know exactly the looks of revulsion you're talking about. But they aren't a reflection of you. They're a reflection of ignorance. People just need to be taught."

"I want to teach drivers to race, not sit around the campfire giving lessons on etiquette and singing 'Kumbaya' with them."

"It doesn't start with a lesson on etiquette. It starts with you knowing your worth."

"He's right," Maddie interrupted. "So many girls I see come and go from the Boss's house. They come already broken. They don't know their worth. They don't know Jesus loves them. He wants to help them. He wants to make them beautiful."

Roni scoffed. "How can you sit there and say Jesus wants to help them when He could take all their pain away in an instant? He could have taken your pain away. So many cry out in pain. They're a hostage to it. He could free them in the blink of an eye."

"He already has." Maddie moved to the edge of the sofa, her hands folded on her knees. "He ransomed us to spend eternity with Him by dying on the cross for our sins. We are free. Free and forgiven."

Roni sneered. "Being forgiven doesn't relieve the pain."

"No, but knowing how valuable you are to God gives you the strength you need to get through it."

Maddie looked to Ethan. "Agent Ethan, I heard you in car. I can tell you for sure, you are forgiven. God doesn't see your guilt. He sees His son standing on all sides of you, claiming you as His and choosing you for something great. Something He planned long ago."

Ethan remained still, and his gaze never left Maddie's.

"Knowing that gives you strength. *Sí*? Knowing God has plans for you gives you strength. He wants to make you beautiful, but that comes only when you stop hiding and learn your worth. Do you believe you are forgiven, Agent Ethan? Will you let Jesus make you worthy?"

Ethan looked at Roni, his eyes imploring her to agree so he could accept Maddie's declaration of forgiveness.

Roni couldn't get on board. "Too many times I cried out to God to take me, and He never answered my prayers." She waved a hand at Ethan. "Do what you want, but honestly, I think you're too hard on yourself. And as for God making you more beautiful, I don't think He'll have too much work to do in that department. Just saying."

Ethan flashed her his electrifying grin. "You like what you see, do you?"

"The fire burned my neck, not my eyes. I know beauty when I see it."

Ethan moved in close to her, his grin sobered into a thin line. "Except beauty comes from here—" He pointed to her head, continuing, "and here." He pointed to her chest, lifting the tail of her scarf to ripple through his large, masculine fingers. "A piece of silk isn't it."

"Roni!" a woman's voice called and Roni exhaled on a hard breath she hadn't realized she'd been holding.

She stepped away from Ethan to find her maid, Cora Daniels, entering through the doorway with Wade and Lacey and Cora's sister. Uncle Clay stepped up behind Cora as she rushed at Roni, arms out. "Oh, I can't believe you're here. I just can't believe it."

Ethan hauled Roni back before Cora made contact. Roni tried to push his arms away, but he held fast.

"Why would it be so hard for you to believe that Roni's here, Ms. Daniels? Could it be because you paid someone to make sure she never returned?"

TWELVE

"Ethan! What do you think you're doing?" Roni swung around to face him. He ignored her shocked and irate expression to keep his eyes on the woman Roni loved as a mother. A woman who could be the enemy within her walls.

Ethan sized up the petite woman, early sixties, chestnut hair with gray at the temples and pulled back into a bun at the nape of her neck. Her yellow blouse and tan pants were crisp and of high quality. She looked as though she could be the owner of the estate and not the hired help.

"You said you were tired of appearances. That means asking the tough questions to get to the truth. If Ms. Daniels loves you like you think she does, then she won't mind."

The maid brought her arms down to her side. "It's all right, Roni. I'll answer whatever you want, Agent Gunn."

Clay rushed forward, stepping in front of the maid. "Oh, this is insane! Cora would never put

Veronica in harm's way. How dare you suggest that she would."

"Clayton." Ms. Daniels put her hand on his forearm and let it linger. One might say even held on as a united front. "I have nothing to hide."

Ethan eyed Roni and saw she, too, watched the friendly hand gesture between the maid and the uncle. There was a closeness between the two that went beyond employer and employee.

"How long has this been going on?" Roni asked. "And don't lie and tell me I'm wrong. That's why you were at his house when I called, isn't it?"

Cora inhaled sharply but quickly regained her regal-like composure. She did remove her hand slowly from Clay's arm and folded her own at her front.

"I told you why she was there," Clay Spencer snarled. "You're crossing the line, missy. What Cora does in her free time is none of your business. You don't own her."

"Own her?" Roni recoiled. She looked to Maddie sitting uneasily on the edge of the sofa. "I think I've had enough of people owning people. It makes me sick."

"Then let her make her own choices, even if you don't agree."

Roni locked gazes with her maid. "You want to retire. Is that what this is about?"

"I just want to hold you right now. I have been

beside myself with fear that I would never see you again. I thank God that you are home and safe. Nothing else matters right now."

Cora stepped forward for Roni again. Roni moved to meet her and took the older woman gently in her arms. It seemed the two melted into each other.

Ethan took in the faces around the room. Everyone except Clay watched with rapt attention and small smiles of understanding. They all knew of the bond between Roni and Cora and respected it as a mother's and child's.

Everyone except Clay Spencer.

Why? Jealousy of their relationship? Did he harbor feelings for Cora all these years and, with Roni in the way, couldn't act on them? Was that the reason he wanted Roni married and moved on? Did it have nothing to do with staying on as CEO for Spencer Speedway and everything to do with a hidden love he could never act upon with her here?

People would do a lot for love.

Some might even be driven to murder after forty years of being deprived of voicing their feelings.

Clayton Spencer had once befriended the man who killed Bobby and Meredith Spencer. Clay moved in to play the part of guardian for Wade and Roni…but was that only for appearances' sake?

Ethan firmed up what this whole scene must

have looked like. Cora Daniels, maid/mother. Clayton Spencer, uncle/father.

For a while, Clay was as close to his dream as he could possibly get, living under the same roof with the woman he loved, raising two wounded children, biding his time until they were grown and moved on, leaving him and Cora in their empty nest.

But there will always be obstacles thrown into the paths of our dreams. And things didn't go as Spencer planned. Clay Spencer wasn't planning on his little Veronica kicking him out when she grew up, instead of leaving herself.

Roni was an expert at avoiding obstacles on the track, but did she know she was her uncle's biggest obstacle in his life, and he had been trying to get around her this whole time?

The two other women in the room stepped up to Cora and Roni. The first to reach for Roni was a small, but tough-looking young woman in her mid-to-late twenties. Her long brown hair was pulled back in a messy ponytail. When she spoke to welcome Roni home, her deep Southern drawl told Ethan she must be Wade's wife, Lacey.

The other woman reached for Cora and they cried together. They were similar in age and Ethan judged by their features that they were sisters. They were obviously close, even though Cora's clothing came from one of those high-class boutiques and the other woman's didn't. It dawned on Ethan that Jared Finlay was Cora's nephew.

Did that make this woman Jared's mother?

"I will need your names," he said to the ladies when they had disengaged and were ready to help him find Roni's enemy. "I'll need to run checks on everyone in this room. Don't take it personal."

The sister stepped up to him, tears streaming down her face, her chin trembling. "You're a federal agent?"

"Yes, ma'am."

"I'm Tanya Finlay." Her voice cracked with more tears choking her words. "I think the person you are looking for is my son."

Cora held her sister's hand for support as she told all she knew about her son. Roni knew Cora's care and love firsthand and wouldn't impede the younger sister offering it to the other, even if Tanya was Jared's mother, and her son might be the one trying to kill Roni. She had to figure no mother wanted her child to grow up to become a killer, and Tanya had done her best in raising Jared given her circumstances in life.

Cora and Tanya grew up down in the village, long before the revitalization of Norcastle took place. Their home was like so many during the decline of the economy: a dreary, run-down reflection of late 19th century factory worker housing. The rows of boxed homes were never more than utilitarian roofs over the workers' heads to begin with, but add years of economic downslide to them, and that was the picture of Cora's and Tanya's childhood.

It was Cora who applied as the Spencer family maid forty years ago when Bobby and Meredith Spencer came to town to open a racetrack that would lift the town out of its economic hole. Jobs by the hundreds became available, and slowly new life spread over Norcastle.

But not over Tanya's household.

While Roni dated Jared, he had shared about his absent father—not much, but enough for her to know Adam Finlay had a gambling problem and was off somewhere looking for his next win. A win he always said would be coming soon.

Roni remembered her uncle Clay kicking him out of the racetrack when she was younger. The Finlay patriarch thought he would provide for his family by running a gambling network at the track and betting on raccs.

Roni had to admit that was one thing she agreed with Uncle Clay about. Spencer Speedway would not be used as a betting track. People came for the love of the sport, not for losing their shirts. It would be a place that would bring families together, not a place that would break them apart.

"Jared left town three days ago. He hasn't checked in," Tanya said.

"We need to call Sylvie." Roni interrupted Ethan's questioning. "We know Jared has my car. We know he tried to kill us at the gas station. We know he did kill whoever was in that helicopter."

"Who's Sylvie?" Ethan asked.

"She's the chief of police."

"I don't think involving the police is what you want right now. Not until you're ready to turn yourself in to the FBI. That will set off all kinds of alarms."

"Sylvie's a friend from the track. I'll call her personal line. She has to know what Jared is capable of."

Tanya turned her head into Cora's neck and cried quietly. Cora soothed her with a hand to her back and to Roni, she cast scolding eyes. "Consider your words, Roni."

"I'm sorry, but there's no way of making this pretty, nor should we. I'm calling Sylvie. At the very least, she should know Norcastle is about to have visitors."

Roni walked to the end table for the handheld, but before she could pick it up, Ethan beat her to it. "No phone. It's tapped."

"And you know this how?" Wade asked.

Ethan's gaze stayed on her. "Because I tapped it."

Uncle Clay reached into his pants pocket and removed his cell. "You can use my phone. Unless you found a way to be listening in on my phone calls, too."

"No, you weren't the suspect."

The room grew quiet with all eyes on Roni.

Wade spoke first. "What exactly do you have on my sister that would cause you to tap her phone?"

"Bank records, emails, a trip to Florida that resulted in the smuggling of people into port… and a relationship with Franco Guerra."

Roni recoiled her hand from Ethan's where it still held hers on the phone. "I never met Guerra before the night he kidnapped me."

"They have a picture of you with him in Florida. You're shaking hands. You have met him before. You may not remember it, but that won't matter in court. And this will go to court. It will take more than my word to clear you of wrongdoing."

"I would remember that sleazy man. Where's the picture? There has to be an explanation."

"I'm sure there is. Especially if someone wanted to make sure you were locked up for a long time." Ethan surveyed the faces in the room. "If anyone knows anything that would clear Roni's name, you have to tell me."

At the heavy silence and disheartened faces, Roni looked at Tanya. "I'm sorry, but if your son did this to me, he will pay dearly."

Tanya produced pleading hands toward Roni. "I'm so sorry, Roni. I don't understand. He loved you."

"No he didn't. He loved the thrill. He loved what I did for him. And when I took that away, he sought retaliation. It's as plain as his driving was before I taught him everything he knows. Without me he's nothing."

"Roni!" Cora raised her voice. "I told you to watch what you say. She is hurting just as much as you. Can't you see that?"

"I don't trust anything I see anymore. Nothing is as it seems." Roni reached for her throat, and for the first time her own scarf, giving the biggest false appearance in the room, felt like a burn all over again. She retracted her hand and held it out for Clay's phone.

"I'm calling Sylvie. She'll know what to do. She'll be able to see the truth through all the lies. Even all the lies in this room."

THIRTEEN

Chief Sylvie Laurent sat at the head of the dining room table, a notepad with all the details she had collected from each person she questioned. She stuck the pencil through her blond hair, pulled back in a tight bun, and closed the pad with a tap.

The dining room chairs were filled, while Ethan remained standing, waiting for the attacks of their pursuers.

The question was who would show their face first?

Would it be Ramsey, looking for retribution for the collapse of his organization? Or would it be Pace, looking to close a case he'd lived and breathed for five years? Or would it be Jared, who at this point had to know he stood on the edge of destruction. That made him more dangerous than Ramsey and Pace combined. He would be desperate.

Ethan searched the faces at the table, landing on the chief's. "Now that you all have caught the chief up, I have a few questions, if you don't mind, Chief Laurent. I'm not from around here and might see the pretty picture of family at the dining room table a bit differently."

Sylvie Laurent gave a wry smile with a knowing nod. "I agree. Go ahead, ask your questions, but I think you'd be surprised in how much I do see."

Ethan liked the no-nonsense chief. She wouldn't be someone claiming jurisdiction and pushing the Fed out. She wanted justice as much as him. Ethan was glad to see Roni had her for a friend. He may be a loner, but he knew friends were important.

Never did he think his own friendship with Pace would be on the line, but things seemed to be taking that course.

To the group, Ethan said, "One or more of you is holding something back. Roni has been set up, and in my experience that happens most times by someone close to the victim. Someone posing as a confidante, a champion even. But that isn't always the case." His gaze stopped on the uncle. "Clay, you have been neither of these things for Roni, your dead brother's child who you raised for him. You have worked hard to make her go away."

Slowly, Clay rose from his chair. "What is this? An ambush against me?"

"You were never Roni's champion. In fact, you

worked hard to marry her to Jared, which would take her from here and leave you in charge of the track. With Wade coming home from the army and Roni not marrying Jared as you had pushed for, you might have found another method to make her go away. Besides the fear of losing your position as CEO at the track, is there another reason why you would want Roni to…disappear?"

"You're out of line!" the uncle yelled, but Ethan didn't miss his quick, fretting glance Cora's way.

Bingo.

Ethan locked gazes with Roni. At her nod, he knew she'd seen it, too. But that didn't stop the pain of betrayal from playing out on her face. She couldn't even look Cora's way.

So Ethan did. "Cora Daniels."

The petite woman straightened in her chair across from Clay, who hadn't taken his seat again. Clay's warning glare spoke louder than his voice. The man had it bad for the family's maid.

But did she feel the same way? Would she have gone along with Clay's schemes if she saw no other way for them to be together?

"Ms. Daniels, you have devoted your life to the Spencer children, Roni in particular. She shared with me how you stepped in and filled the role of mother to her. You were more than a maid to them."

"How could I not?" she asked quietly, offering a sad smile at Roni. "The poor child was in so much pain and didn't know why. She cried for her mommy while she couldn't even cry out in pain from her burns. I had to be a voice for her." Cora's throat clogged at her surfacing memories. "I..." She swallowed hard. "I couldn't walk away."

Ethan grappled with the image Cora painted of Roni as a child. He had to push it aside to stay focused. Stopping his legs from making a beeline for her was the hardest part. He had an overwhelming need to pull her into his arms and push his face into her neck, promising her that her voice would never be silenced again.

Ethan shook his head and pushed out his response to Cora. "Even if that meant you lived up on this isolated mountain raising children that would never be yours, limiting your chances of ever having a family of your own."

Roni inhaled sharply. "Oh, Cora, I never thought of that. I'm so sorry."

"Nothing to be sorry for, honey. I made that decision all on my own. You were a child in need of a mother. I couldn't turn away from you. I don't regret anything."

Ethan wasn't finished yet. "You were practically a child yourself when you came on board here, correct?"

"I was twenty. I'm sixty years old now."

"Commendable. Thank you. But why haven't you retired? I'm sure you're paid well and could live comfortably for the rest of your life."

"The Spencers have always blessed me financially, and with living here all these years, I have saved enough to enjoy the rest of my days quite nicely."

"But…"

"But I'm not ready to retire. Maybe in a few years we'll revisit the discussion."

"Revisit? As in retirement is something you have brought up?"

"Sure, but we decided it wasn't time yet."

Ethan watched Roni's gaze drop to her hands in her lap. "We? You mean you and Roni decided?"

"Yes. It's only the two of us living here now." She smiled warmly at the only daughter she'd ever had. It all appeared to be copasetic. Nothing to see here.

Or was there?

"You encouraged Roni to take Jared under her wing. I take it you were happy about the engagement?"

"Of course."

"Can you tell me what your life would have been like for you if she had left here for the racing circuit with her husband?"

The woman laughed. "Lonely, I'm sure, but I would have been happy for her." She patted her sister's hand beside her and said, "Jared is a good man. He is. He's lost right now, and he needs our prayers. I never would have believed he would be capable of such crimes, but I suppose we all have our limits before our sinful natures come out."

"Are you saying you think Roni pushed your nephew's limits too far?"

Cora lost her pasted-on smile. She swallowed again, now looking nervous of where this conversation was going. She knew the accolades of all her sacrifices had come to an end. She cleared her throat and shifted in her seat.

Roni stood. "Perhaps it would be easier for all if I left the room. Please, everyone, this is no time to hold anything back. Even if you think it doesn't amount to anything, or you're afraid you'll hurt me in sharing. I'll be a lot more hurt if you don't." To Ethan, she said, "I'm going to go freshen up. It's been a long few days. Come on, Maddie. I'll show you your room."

At his nod, the two women took their leave around the corner. Roni's boots could be heard tapping up the flight of stairs in the main entrance foyer.

When Roni was out of earshot, he knew the group was out of hers. "All right, Ms. Daniels, you heard Roni. Hold nothing back. Tell us how you really feel."

The maid couldn't look at anyone at the table. A sigh of resignation curled her shoulders in. "I was disappointed in how Roni publicly humiliated Jared. Yes, he wronged her, but two wrongs just make more to be fixed. That's why God commands us to forgive. It's not just for the person who did the wrongdoing. It's also for the person who's been wronged. It's a time when that person can draw closer to God to depend on Him for comfort and strength."

"Like you do for your sister," Ethan said. "I can see she depends on you."

Tanya jerked in her seat, aware that the conversation had just switched to her turn.

Everyone at the table became aware that they were all under scrutiny and would have to answer questions that went below the surface for things they didn't want to face themselves.

The place where the truth lay.

He continued, "Cora, you asked Roni to teach Jared to race and encouraged her to help him financially for your sister, correct? Did you feel guilty about living in so much luxury when your sister struggled so much?"

Cora frowned and glanced Tanya's way. "She's had it hard. I've tried to help her when I can. All I asked was for Roni to teach him what she knows. I had no idea he would be so successful, but yes, I was delighted to see he had such wonderful talent and was able to help his family's finances. I imagine Jared is crushed that he's lost that ability to provide for his family like during his winning success."

"Are you saying you condone Jared's actions? People died, and Roni could have, too."

"Of course not. Jared will have to pay for all he's done."

"Not if I don't have factual evidence that will show Jared set Roni up. Right now the FBI has enough on her to put her away for a long time. And if the FBI doesn't grab her first, there are two other—more dangerous—people who will. I need something that will stop the FBI from pursuing her. Something that will turn their efforts to aiding her instead. Mrs. Finlay, I am going to need to get into Jared's home. Do you have a key?"

Tanya startled at the question. "Actually, Jared's been living with me since he was dropped by his sponsors. He had to give up his apartment for a while. Just until he can land another big sponsor. So, yes, I can let you into my house. There's not much there, though. He really only sleeps there, and I haven't seen him in days."

"Yes, that's because he's been out trying to kill us."

A piercing scream reached the group from somewhere above them.

"Roni," Ethan and Wade said at the same time. Both men raced for the open doorway.

"Promise, stay by Lacey." Wade commanded his dog to guard his wife and bolted from the room.

Ethan looked back at the chief of police. He didn't have to say a word. Sylvie Laurent was already on her feet, retrieving her weapon and giving orders for the group to retreat to their safe room.

Ethan followed Wade out through the great room and into the foyer. The stairway curved up to an open landing that led off to a hall of closed doors. Without Wade, Ethan would have had only Roni's bloodcurdling screams to guide him to the right room. He could have lost precious seconds in reaching her before they stopped—or were stopped.

Tense pain gripped his chest with each thud of his boots on the wood floors. Fear choked him more than when he went up against Guerra and Ramsey.

Her piercing screams grew louder as they neared the last door. Wade reached for the knob and found it locked.

Ethan lifted his boot. One kick splintered the wooden door and opened the entrance for them. He climbed through, tripping on a jagged piece of wood with his leg behind him, but nothing that held him back.

Get to Roni, echoed through his mind. And nothing or nobody would stop him.

The door opened to a short hall and lounge area. On the other side of the sofa, the door to the bedroom was open and Roni's screams bounced off the walls around him. He reached her room and fell back a step.

Roni sat in the middle of the floor with arms circling her bent legs pulled up close to her chin. She continued to wail, but not from any physical threat.

The threat surrounding her was an emotional one. One his gun would do nothing to stop.

Everywhere the eye landed, the same eight-by-ten picture showed. An image of some car engulfed in flames. Ethan only gave them a quick glance, the woman beside herself on the floor taking precedence.

Ethan reached her in a sprint. His knees hit the floor as he grabbed her upper arms. "Roni, look at me. Are you hurt?"

She kept her head down, eyes shut.

Wade walked over to where curtains waved into the room.

The window was open.

Someone had gone through it to put these pictures up. But were they still in the house? Had they hurt Roni?

Ethan shook her to engage. "Roni, sweetheart, I need to know if you're hurt."

"She's not hurt, but she's hurting," Wade said with one of the pictures in his hand. He'd removed it from the wall next to the window. He looked up from it to scan the room in a circle. "These are pictures of the car crash."

"*Your* car crash? From when you were kids?"

"That's our family's Mercedes. I would remember it anywhere. I pretty much live with this image in my mind every day and night."

Ethan could see the paleness spreading over Wade's face. "Stay with me, Wade. Your sister needs you."

"Right." Wade gave one last look at the picture in his hand and threw it to the floor. "Let's get her out of here. The images are tormenting her."

"I would say both of you." Ethan cradled Roni in his arms and immediately she latched both arms around his neck in a death grip. He carried her through the doorway and met Maddie entering the other room, her hair wet from a shower and her eyes wide with fright.

"I heard her screaming. I couldn't get here. Is she all right?"

"Just scared," Ethan assured her.

Sylvie stepped out of the room behind them with her radio in her hand. "I need to call this in. I won't mention Roni being here just yet. It's a break-in and the perpetrator could still be out there. I need my men on this before we have a full-fledged situation on this mountain."

"I think it's too late to stop that." Ethan knew what he had to do. "You can call your men, but I'm also calling mine."

"I thought you were afraid Roni wouldn't be treated fairly by the agent in charge. How has that changed?"

Ethan replied over Roni's shoulder. She held

him so tight that he felt her body trembling against him. "I figure being treated fairly won't matter if she's dead. Plus they'll have to question the setup when they see the room. Maybe it will be enough for them to look in another direction."

Wade opened a walk-in closet with his gun ready. Hangers of clothes scraped along a bar as he jerked them for views behind them. At finding nobody, he said, "I'm going to check the house to see if our company is still inside. Roni should join the others in the safe room," he said.

"I remember how to get there," Ethan confirmed. "And then I'll join you."

"No. Stay with her." Wade nodded to the back of his sister still clinging to Ethan. "I've never seen Roni need anyone. It looks like I was wrong. She does. She just hides it well." With that, Wade retreated, tensed and at the ready.

"I'll secure the scene for my men to process," Sylvie said. "Maybe we'll find a print on one of those photos."

Roni let out a whimper at the mention of them. Ethan rubbed her back to soothe her. "You're safe, sweetheart. Pictures can't hurt you."

"There were more," she muffled against his neck.

"More? In another room?"

She shook her head. "A few months ago. When I told the world about Jared. I also called the wedding off in the public statement. I...I came home and the picture…it was nailed to my front door. I tore it to shreds in an instant. It felt like I was being burned all over again."

"I would imagine whoever put it there knew it would have that effect on you. It's a warning, I'm sure. But it will not come to fruition with me by your side. I promise."

Roni lifted her face from his neck. Petrified eyes implored his. Dried streaks of tears marred her face and her scarf was wet and matted. Her scars peeked out from behind, reminding him she'd already endured this pain once. A need inside him arose to make sure she never did again.

"Why are you helping me? Why do you care?" she asked and he didn't have an answer to give.

Ethan could have thrown out that he was responsible for her safety. She was a civilian in his assignment. He'd nearly lost a civilian before while he worked undercover and vowed never to again. The answer would have been a legit one to give her.

But it would have been another appearance covering up the truth, and that was what Roni didn't want more of.

But what was the truth?

"When I first came on in this assignment, I read your file." He spoke at a slow pace, soothing he hoped. "I thought you were beautiful. But I also thought that's all you were. After meeting you I saw the truth. You were more than beautiful. You were strong and smart and brave. I saw the file had you all wrong. I saw *I* had you all wrong."

Roni's trembling began to subside, with only flinches of residual aftermath tremors twitching her muscles involuntarily and sporadically. Her eyes still waited for the answer to her question.

The one stuck in the back of his throat.

Had he lost the focus of his job? Pace would say so. He would say the flashy woman had blindsided him. And maybe she did, but his mission was still the same.

"I want to find the truth, Roni. And it's not just to get the bad guys anymore. The lies we believe about ourselves are our biggest shackles. They hold us back, and they hold us down. I want to know who I would be if I didn't believe them anymore. And I want to know who you would be."

Roni shrunk back. "Me? I know who I am."

"I know you think you do. But ask yourself why you just flipped out over a bunch of paper and ink."

Her gaze went to Maddie, who had taken one of the overstuffed chairs and watched them intently. She frowned. "All right. So maybe I do remember that day more than I admit. But it was better to forget it. There was no reason to relive it over and over again like Wade does. I've seen how it changed him. How he hurts. If I could forget it, I would be strong enough for both of us. I would be able to help him."

"And have you?"

No answer came, but eventually, Roni gave a shake to her head. "No matter how much I tried, no, I couldn't. Uncle Clay has been the only one to help my brother."

"And that must irk you big-time."

She huffed. "You have no idea."

"It was probably what drove the wedge deep between the two of you in the first place. Don't you think?"

Roni smirked her wry lips and looked up to him with cynical eyes beneath long lashes. "So this is what you had in mind when you said you wanted to uncover the lies. Psychoanalyze Roni Spencer until she embraced the people who have let her down in life? I didn't know FBI agents were also shrinks."

"We're not. We're cops, but being a cop is more than serving and protecting. It's understanding the human psyche. And right now you've got some people against you that I need to understand."

Ethan pushed her back and got to his feet. He extended a hand for her to take.

"We need to get you to the safe room. It's time I called Pace...if he's still alive." Ethan mumbled the last under his breath.

She frowned. "I suppose you're right. It doesn't

look like my family is about to confess to setting me up, unless you got something out of them after I left the room."

"No. I have more questions than ever."

"That's what I figured. A house full of secrets is what this place is."

They walked out of the room and down the hall to the stairs, Maddie following.

"It must be very lonely for you here," Ethan said.

"Lonely? Nah, Cora and I keep each other company." Roni reached for Maddie's hand. "And now we'll have Maddie, too."

"But they're not your real family," Ethan pointed out. At her look of defense, he raised a hand to stop her. "Don't shoot, I get it. Pace is to me what Cora is to you. They're our chosen family. But why is it, Roni, that we felt the need to replace our real family?"

"Easy. Because we weren't good enough for them."

Ethan guided the way down two flights of stairs until they reached the lowest level. A false wall with shelves moved aside with the code Wade had shown him earlier. A vault door appeared behind it, and he put a second code in to unlatch it.

It opened smoothly with a click and swung wide on soundless hinges.

The room was more than a room. It was a small

apartment with enough to live on for months if they had to. If Roni's parents hadn't been murdered, he would have thought they were really paranoid to have built this place.

Cora jumped up from her place on a simple sofa and met Roni with a hug. The maid brought her over to the other ladies to sit, but Maddie lingered behind with Ethan.

At her look of unease at the heavy door, he saw her apprehension of being locked in. She gave a weak smile when she saw he watched her.

"It's just for a little while, Maddie. Until I meet with Pace. After that I'll be back down to unlock it. It will all be over tonight."

Ethan hoped Pace was still alive to make that statement true. He hoped instead of arresting Roni, though, she would be put in protection. He would have to do a lot of convincing for that outcome, but before he shut the door, he said to Maddie, "Would you pray?"

The young woman's lips turned up in a bigger smile. "I haven't stopped," she said. "For either of you."

"Thank you. Because I'm about to go up against the only family I have, and I don't know what happens when you lose your chosen family. Something tells me it will hurt a whole lot worse."

"God chose you, Agent Ethan. He even fought to the death and back for you. I imagine your pain won't even come close to how He feels when we don't choose Him back."

"He loves us that much, huh? I see I have some rethinking to do about my relationship with Him. After tonight that could be the only one I have left."

"I've been there. When it was God and me, only. He was always with me. Sure, there were times I doubted it, but I know now He never left me. And He hasn't left you either, Agent Ethan Gunn."

"Ethan. Just Ethan. To be honest, Gunn isn't my real name. It's my undercover name."

"Interesting." Maddie's head tilted. "My real name is Magdalena. I guess we both have a part of us we need to let out."

A sick laugh escaped his lips. "That might not be a good idea."

"Then we're no different than Roni. She just uses fancy silks to cover up her darkest places."

With that, Maddie pulled the inside lever of the vault closed herself, on her terms, but leaving Ethan standing there to realize his undercover lifestyle was no different than the scarves Roni lived under.

But Ethan Gunn was a man of intrigue and danger.

Ethan Rhodes was a nobody from South LA. He didn't have a life worth saving.

Roni's words of not being good enough for her family hit home. But Ethan Rhodes wasn't good enough even for himself.

FOURTEEN

"Standing by the door is not going to bring him back faster," Cora said, stepping up behind Roni. Promise also stood post by the door waiting for Wade to return. Roni rubbed the soft coat of fur behind the dog's ear. This was the first time the dog brought her comfort, typically only concerned for her handler's.

Roni checked the clock above the stove again. One minute later from the last time she checked. She sighed in frustration. "Ethan's been gone for two hours. Why is this taking so long? His team should have been here by now. This isn't good. His boss must not be willing to work with him. Or he was in that helicopter and is dead. Ethan would be devastated to lose his friend, even if the guy thought I was guilty. What if Pace is dead and Ethan doesn't know who to trust at the Bureau?"

Cora placed an assuring hand on her shoulder. "If that's the case, then Ethan won't reveal you're down here."

"But what will that mean for him?" Roni cried out.

Cora's mouth dropped on a slight inhale; a smile slowly followed.

"How can you smile about this? He's putting himself in danger with the FBI. That's nothing to smile about!"

Cora's smile continued to blossom. "And you're thinking of him first."

Roni recoiled. "Thanks a lot, Cora. I do think of people before myself, you know." She glanced over at the ladies watching the television to pass the time.

Lacey, Tanya and Maddie all stared at the screen, but none appeared to be paying much attention. Lacey kept glancing at the door, worried for her husband. Tanya was a mother whose son had gone off the deep end. Her mind had to come to grips with that. And Maddie. Poor Maddie didn't know who to trust. It didn't matter how many times Roni assured her she was safe here and welcome to call this place home, the day may never come when she not only accepted that offer, but believed it.

"I'm giving Maddie a home, aren't I?" Roni said under her breath to Cora. "I'm thinking of her first. I resent you saying such a thing to me, Cora."

"Well, you didn't think of Jared before you smeared his name on the air for the world to see."

Roni stood speechless before the woman who always offered her loving and kind words. The woman who would sing to her as a child when she was in excruciating pain. She knew the agony then, how did she not see the pain Jared caused her when they dated?

And why did Cora's opinion of her hurt so much more than Uncle Clay's and Wade's?

Because Cora was her chosen family.

"I suppose that's what you would see," Roni resigned herself to saying. Tears pricked her eyes, and she squeezed them back with a press of her eyelids. "And that's my own fault for allowing the world to see only what they wanted to see." Roni touched the scarf at her neck, absently feeling for any visible scars above the edge. Ethan urged her to take it off, but he didn't realize she wore these scarves not for herself, but because she knew people didn't want to see her ugliness. She wore them because she *did* think of everyone else first.

But then that would make her just as guilty of appearances as everyone else. Just as guilty as her uncle's appearance to support her. Just as guilty as Jared's appearance to love her. Just as guilty as Maddie's traffickers, who lied to her family and told them she would have a better life if they sold her. Everything appears to be beautiful and perfect, but what is it all hiding?

If her reaction to all those photos in her room

was any indication, perhaps her scarves weren't to make her burns easy on the eyes for outsiders, but rather to protect herself from remembering how she got them in the first place.

Roni lowered her voice and asked, "Do you remember that night, Cora?"

Cora scanned the living area to see who might be listening. "I'm assuming you mean the crash."

Roni nodded, her eyes downcast. Did she really want to try to pull those images out from some place in her mind?

"I wasn't there, but you and Wade said things that tore my heart out."

"*I* said things?"

Cora paused. "You were deliriously in pain and couldn't speak for a while, but yes, eventually when you were able, you talked of the fire, mostly in your sleep. You cried for your mom, and you called out for Luke. You cried a lot for Luke."

Roni chewed on her inner cheek, her arms crossed in front of her. "I wonder why."

"He was beside you in the rear seat. I always thought when Wade pulled you out of the car, your last view was of Luke. Your little three-year-old mind didn't understand why you were leaving him behind in the fire."

"I don't remember any of this. I only remember reaching for my mom, then waking up in the hospital and finding you beside me. I don't remember the crash, and I barely remember Luke at all."

"Our minds have the ability to protect us sometimes by forgetting. But trust me when I say, you were beside yourself with worry for your baby brother. Oh, how I ached for you, and then one day you just stopped calling for him. It was like you finally knew that he was gone and he wasn't coming back."

"What if he's not really gone, Cora? We know that the accident report was switched out for our protection against my parents' enemies, so they would never go looking for Luke. It had to look like he was confirmed dead. But his body was nowhere near the crash site. Maybe I knew he was still alive and needed our help. Maybe that's why I was beside myself with worry."

"Are you up for rehashing the crash now? You've never wanted to before. Why now?"

Roni thought of all the pictures tacked to her bedroom walls. "Because someone's using the fire to get to me. Someone who knows me better than I know myself." Roni paused to collect her thoughts. So many new things to consider. "Something I learned while I was escaping from Ramsey's is that I've spent my entire life since I was three years old avoiding another fire. My expertise in racing had been all about evading death again and again and again. And someone out there knows it and wants me to know they know it. They know my fear and will use it against me."

"Then let's pray Agent Gunn convinces his boss to protect you."

"Pray?" Roni glanced at Maddie, sitting quietly on a chair. Her hands were clasped and her eyes were closed. Maddie, who lost the only life she had ever known kept her faith through it all. Could Roni have such faith? "I know you've always prayed for me, but honestly, I never wanted anything to do with God. Not since I prayed for Him to take me and He didn't."

Cora's eyebrows reached for the ceiling. "Take you? You mean after the crash?"

"No, I mean after my last surgery. I was getting older and aware of the looks my burns garnered. I saw the hopelessness of ever being whole again in the eyes of the world. What's ironic is I've had ample opportunity to end it all on the track. I think my fear of fire is what has kept me alive."

"God has kept you alive. He has a purpose for you. Perhaps you'll soon find what that is, and life will look differently for you. But that can only happen when you are open to Him working in your life. You have to let Him take the wheel, sweetie."

"If I wouldn't let Ethan, how will I let God? And speaking of Ethan, what is taking so long?"

"Whatever it is, he needs our prayers. Will you pray with me?" Cora placed her aged hand on Roni's youthful one. The contrast staggered her. It looked so much older than she remembered.

Blue veins were beginning to rise up beneath her thinner skin. When had the aging process raced ahead for Cora? Had it been going on for a while, and Roni had been ignoring the signs so she wouldn't have to face the truth? Soon Cora would retire and leave the Spencer home. There was no longer any way to blindfold herself from this fact.

But still, Roni took Cora's hand and closed her eyes to the way the frailer bones in her hand felt so light in her youthfully strong grasp. Earlier today, Roni had asked for the blinders to come off, to see through the appearances once and for all. How could she now close her eyes to the fact that Cora had every right to spend her retirement years on some beach somewhere being waited on after her many years of service to the Spencer family?

"Dear heavenly Father—" Cora began "—we come before You as Your adopted children in need of Your perfect wisdom and help. You have told us that we are to come to You with all our petitions, and You will hear us and provide…"

Roni squeezed Cora's hands at the mention of being God's adopted children. The thought grabbed her attention. For so long she had thought of Cora as her adopted mother, if not in name, in perception. But always, Roni wondered if Cora reciprocated that notion.

Her maid's requests to retire said no.

"Please, Lord, we ask You to intervene in this situation and clear Your child Roni's name from all wrongdoing a naysayer has created against her. And please be with Agent Gunn as he meets with his boss. Please keep him safe in this dangerous profession You have him in. I can't imagine the danger an undercover agent faces daily. You've brought him this far. Will You please see him through to the end. However that end looks to Your will."

The word *end* stuck in Roni's head. How would it all end? And how could she hide away in this room and let it all happen?

The pictures had thrown her, but was that what someone wanted to happen?

Was this a trap? And she fell right into it?

Roni's heart rate skyrocketed at where her thoughts led. Without Ethan fighting with her on her side, she would have no one to vouch for her. She would be put away for a long time.

"I need to get out of here," Roni announced. She headed for the vault door and pushed the code to unlock the bar.

"What's changed?" Cora followed on her heels. The rest of the women jumped to their feet.

"It's another setup. Ethan's in danger."

"Are you sure?"

"He's the only one who can testify that I was set up. Without him, I'm done for. He was supposed to arrest me and hasn't. He's become a nuisance to someone's plan. Someone knew how to break me down to get us separated. That could be for one reason only." Roni pulled the bar up and the vault opened without a sound. She swung the door wide and pushed the bookcase wall aside just as rapid gunfire tore through the house somewhere above the stairs.

Cora latched herself on to Roni. "Don't go up there," she pleaded.

"They're after Ethan. I have to. He should be the one in this room. He's in as much danger as I am. More, because they'll just shoot to kill. He thinks they're here to talk. They don't want to talk, they want *me*. And *he's* in the way!"

Roni took Cora's hand from her arm and disengaged her desperate grip.

Lacey approached them, carrying a handgun like the one Ethan had shown her how to use. "You can't go out there alone."

"I won't let you join me, Lacey. Wade told me you two are expecting. I don't need a fourth person gunning for me if something were to happen to you and your child."

Lacey rolled her brown eyes in her dainty little face. Roni would never tell Lacey she thought her dainty. She would end up on the floor, knowing Lacey's defense moves. Her sister-in-law shook her head with pursed lips. "Figures he would tell you, but you should know me by now. I don't sit around waiting. I go unless God tells me no."

"Consider this your no, then. You're not leaving this room."

Blasts wrenched through the house again. All the women jolted and paled at the sound. What was happening to their men out there?

"What are you going to do?" Lacey asked.

"Lead them away from here. They want me? They can catch me."

"Here, take the gun." Lacey put the weapon in Roni's hand before she could say no. "I said I wouldn't let you go out there alone. I meant it. If it's not me by your side, then a sidearm it will be. I won't take your no for this."

Roni let the gun become comfortable in her hand. She'd held guns before but never had an affinity for them, especially after Wade joined the army and his PTSD injury worsened. She didn't want the weapon around the house. Somehow they worried her and caused her to worry for him. Another reason Lacey was perfect for him. She knew the guns weren't a threat to her husband. They were just a piece of metal. His threats came from a place that couldn't be held and touched. But somehow Lacey had breached his wall and done what Roni never could for her brother.

Roni swung an arm around Lacey and pulled her in close. "I am so grateful for you. I know I don't say it enough, but I am. I love you, Lacey, and I'm so thankful for the love you give to Wade.

Forgive me for being so selfish and not saying so sooner."

"Nothing to forgive. I already knew how you felt. I also know you think Wade deserted you. Please know he never wanted you to feel that way. It was never you." Tears sprang to Lacey's eyes. "Never."

Tears filled Roni's eyes at what Lacey was sharing with her. In this moment, her sister-in-law wanted her to know Wade had not rejected her. His own painful trauma was the cause that divided brother from sister.

"He loves you so much," Lacey confirmed. "It hurts him knowing he hurt you, but he was young and broken. He didn't know how else to handle his pain without leaving. Even if that meant leaving you behind."

Roni swallowed hard and felt the wetness of her tears spill toward the corner of her lips. She stepped back and swiped them away with the palm of her hand.

A glance around the room showed Lacey and Cora crying and Tanya and Maddie pressing their lips in understanding of the situation. They both knew the debilitating power rejection had on a person. They'd both lived with their own.

"I'm going to get to the cars and make sure they know it's me. I'll lead them away from here, but until you know it's safe, please stay in here." She eyed Lacey particularly. "I mean it. Stay…here."

At Lacey's nod, Roni left the women behind to carry out her plan of action.

Bullets smashed into walls above the stairs. Glass could be heard shattering. And she was about to run straight into the thick of it.

No longer would she be avoiding the line of fire. She would be taking the first step in.

FIFTEEN

The crystal chandelier in the front foyer took a stray bullet that missed its mark.

Ethan.

The crash of each falling piece smashing into the wood floor shook him where he crouched for cover. A quick recount of the last split seconds confirmed the bullet had been meant for him.

He had been pressed against the wall, approaching the double front doors. The slender windows on either side would tell him who had come calling, but before he could determine the visitor's identity, the side windows shattered to pieces with a round of rapid fire.

Ethan hit the deck, but the bullets that embedded into the wall he had been pressed against proved he was the target.

He was being taken out. There was no doubt about it. But by whom?

Ethan pressed his pants pocket for the cell

phone Wade had given him. He redialed for the third time the number for Pace.

Still no answer.

Was that because he was dead?

Or because it was his boss who'd ordered the takedown?

Did Pace see it a necessary maneuver in order to get to Roni? He would know that Ethan would die protecting her. That he would take a bullet for her if it meant keeping a civilian alive under his investigation.

But Roni wasn't here.

For Pace to take him out without the civilian in the vicinity, he had to believe Ethan had gone rogue. Or had some other reason for keeping her alive.

Duty had always been the driving force in keeping with his responsibilities for the innocent, but duty never caused the hovering sense of panic that had him second-guessing his every move. One wrong move and he might lose his civilian.

His brain tripped over the word *civilian*. It didn't feel like the correct word to describe Roni. Words like *friend, comrade* and *pal* also didn't work either.

Those just made him feel…bitter.

Here he was sitting on the pristine floors of a fortress that belonged to one of the classiest women he'd ever met. It reminded him of how different their lives were.

His whole apartment could fit into this foyer. Not that he was ever there. He lived undercover, one investigation to the next. The Bureau knew any job could be handed to him, and he wouldn't bat an eye. A month under, a year under, an undeterminable length that could take years all meant more time as Ethan Gunn. No matter the job, he was their man. And they saw him as a man who took each job by the horns. A man in charge.

Roni only saw him as a sidekick.

It was as though she saw through the facade at the real man behind the mask. Ethan Gunn was a fake. Take off his cover, and he was a kid from the hood. His expertise amounted to stealing and cloning cars. Even Guerra had said he'd never seen a better thief. The man didn't know the half of it. That came from practice, and lots of it.

Ethan didn't want Roni to ever know. He wasn't even worthy to be her sidekick, never mind her... what? He was back to finding a word suitable to describe what Roni was to him.

Another round of bullets shattered windows in the dining room. At what point did the shooter or shooters come through them? He prepared to spring up for the ambush, his gun ready for when they did. He trusted Wade to guard the back of the house and alert him by text if they were breached. Clay and Sylvie had the second floor in case they had a climber.

Movement to his left caught his eye. He swung his gun in that direction to take aim at the intruder.

Confusion turned to outright seething anger in less than a second.

"Get down!" he yelled as he stood from his hiding place to dive for the woman under his charge.

Multiple rounds spewed around him in all directions. Thuds and shattered glass wherever the bullets found a place.

Ethan collided into Roni at full force, sending them both skidding across the smooth floors. Bullets hit the floor off to his right. On his knees, he shoved her to the left, behind a fancy chair and side table.

Ethan pushed in close to shield Roni's body with his. His chest rose and fell in rapid repetition, his voice box clogged with pent-up anger. All he could do was wrap his arms around her and squeeze the rage out of himself before it consumed him.

Never had he felt such an emotion. He wasn't even sure if it was rage. It was more like a feeling one might get standing on a precipice of total loss.

His heart clenched. His lungs seized. His brain saw red. His eyes watered up.

"Why?" He managed to break the choke hold around his vocal cords for that one word.

"They want *me*, Ethan. And they know they have to kill you to get to me." Roni shook her head against his cheek. "I've allowed this long enough. I'm grateful for all you've done to keep me safe, but I cannot allow you to give your life for me."

Ethan lifted his face to stare into the wide blue eyes of Veronica Spencer. "You can't stop me."

"Yes, I can," she replied.

Something hard pushed into Ethan's rib cage. It took only a second to remember the glimpse of the gun Roni held before he took her down to the floor.

The fear in her big round eyes told him she would never shoot him, but that didn't mean the trigger wouldn't get pulled accidently in fright. Another spray of bullets could cause her to jerk and pull it.

Ethan reached between them and moved the barrel away from him. Her hand went limp as tears pooled in her eyes. He easily took the gun from her and placed it beside them just as her tears spilled and she let out a wail.

She latched her arms around his neck and trembled in his arms. "I'm so sorry. I would never...I just...I don't want you to die because of me. Let me lead them away from here. It's me they want. Please, Ethan, let me go."

"Shh." He consoled her rising pained speech of selflessness, feeling her streams of tears against his cheeks. He kissed her ear. "It's okay, Roni.

I thank you for thinking of me, but this is what I do."

Her head shook back and forth, and he lifted his face to hers. Inches from her elegant face even in the onslaught of angst. He'd never seen anyone more beautiful. The fact that she meant to protect him made her even more so.

His heart swelled. "No one has ever done anything like that for me. I'm humbled, but you need to let me do my job."

"You didn't sign up to take a bullet meant for the criminal. You protect innocent people, not the guilty."

"You're not guilty."

She lifted her trembling chin. "How do you know? You saw the pictures. I've been lying to you this whole time. I'm guilty. I'm guilty of it all."

Ethan paused for a brief second at her turn-around confession. "All of it, you say?"

"Yes. You've been protecting a crook."

"And trafficker?"

She swallowed hard but nodded once.

"Stop it, Roni. Just stop it."

"No, you stop protecting me. Right now, Ethan Gunn, you stop—"

Ethan slammed his lips down on hers. He meant it at first to silence her crazy request. What she was asking of him was insane. Didn't she understand he would die for her?

No. How could she? He didn't even grasp the weight of that himself.

But with her lips beneath his, moving in accord with him, opening to him, she had to know something he didn't know. Was this her kiss goodbye?

Not if he had anything to say about it. She wasn't losing him that easy. He was a tail she wouldn't be breaking away from.

Ethan slanted his face to pull her in as close as possible, demanding she accept him as something more than her protector. His fingers twined into her gloriously silky red hair, his palm cupping the back of her head to hold her and guide her in their kiss, a symbol of his need to hold her and guide her in their everyday life.

Roni fisted her hands against his chest, twisting his shirt. He felt her strength but wouldn't let her push him away like she wanted to push him out of his job to protect her.

But his job description did not include kissing her.

Abruptly, Ethan pulled apart from her. Their lips were still close, but only their breathing mingled.

She searched his eyes as he knew he searched hers for what this might be between them.

Friends? Comrades? *Pals?*

No. Whatever was between them went way beyond any of those terms.

Ethan had never felt so scared in all his life.

Not even the bullets pummeling her home stood up against the fear of what Roni could do to him. She could very well shatter everything he knew to be true. That solo or no-go was just as much of a farce as his name.

More than ever, Roni needed to escape.

And not just from the assortment of evildoers who had finally caught up to her.

Ethan Gunn stood on the threshold of breaching more than her home's walls. But the damage he could leave behind trumped any pain Jared had ever caused. Something told Roni she would be the one left in the dust, spinning her wheels, and this time, there would be no one to blame but herself.

With Jared, the blame was obvious. His words and actions were abusive and selfish. Ending their relationship came easy.

Nothing would be easy with Ethan.

Roni swallowed hard at the intensity shooting from his eyes. Their chests rose and fell in the same rhythm that spelled havoc and...*fear* for them both.

"Just let me go, Ethan. And this will end right now. It won't go any further. We both know it can't."

She bit her lower lip, tasting him there and fitting the sweet flavor of tenderness to memory.

Never did she want to forget how close she'd come to something that many never see in a lifetime.

Never did she want to forget the way she felt in his arms when he held her with such purpose. His hand behind her head guided her. His other hand trailed down her arm with a light touch.

The flashing red lights of her mind alerted her to dangerous roads ahead.

As though the shooters outside knew of her approaching peril, a lull of gunfire changed to formidable silence.

Ethan was touching her arm. The light fabric of her blouse covered her scars there, but it still put her on alert. His fingers had trailed down from her other scarred place. The place where he had held her during their kiss was her neck.

Ethan's hand had been on her neck.

Panic flooded through every muscle in Roni's body. Her hands where she had bunched his shirt in their kiss became a force to push back humiliation.

He'd touched her scars.

She pushed harder.

"I know what you're thinking, Roni."

"I told you nobody touches me there." She attempted to kick out from his grasp.

"Well, maybe I'm not nobody to you." His lips thinned as though the idea made him just as distressed.

And his hand swept the rest of the way down

her arm at lightning speed until he found her re-
pelling hands. One flick and he had her wrist in
his grasp.

"You're right. You are something to me."

"I don't think this is the time to have this conversation. Confessions under fire don't stick."

"It's nothing I haven't said before." She curled
her lips as though Ethan was a bug under a mi-
croscope.

"And what is that?"

Roni gritted her teeth, knowing what she had
to say. "You're somebody who's just along for the
ride. And that's all you'll ever be. Don't forget it."

Ethan gave a bitter laugh and shook his head.
"That's what you think. Sweetheart, I've been in
the driver's seat from the word *go*. Nothing happened that I didn't allow. Don't you forget *that*."

Before she could say another word, he had her
pulled up and out from their hiding place. He
dragged her behind him at a fast clip toward the
back of the house.

"Where are we going?" she called, ducking her
head when a smattering of gunshots restarted outside. The Norcastle PD was out there. How long
could they hold these people back? They had to
be surrounded themselves.

Please, God, protect them.

The prayer, however simple, stumped her.
Why now? He'd already proven He didn't answer her prayers.

She had no time to squander thinking up a reason for reaching out to God because Ethan's next action stumped her even more.

They reached the back of the house where a bench chest and coat hooks above were situated. He lifted the bench, and she expected him to tell her to climb in.

Any normal person would.

Except Ethan wasn't any normal person, no matter what she just told him.

He grabbed a few boots from the chest and tossed them to the floor. Then he reached in and lifted the bottom board up.

A narrow, steep stairway lay open for them.

Roni inhaled in shock. Not because she didn't know about the secret passageway. She knew about them all. Her mother had her reasons when designing this house and made sure her children knew about every exit. But Roni's shock was because Ethan knew about them.

"How?" she asked as he pushed her in and followed her.

As soon as they were inside, Ethan pulled the cover down, putting them into total darkness.

Roni stepped down carefully a few steps and listened to the muffled gunfire retreat the farther she went. Or perhaps that was because her mind blared louder with fathomless reason of how Ethan could have known about her mother's escape routes.

"You ask how?" he said, close to her ear. "You must not have believed me when I said I've been in the driver's seat since the word *go*. I know about them all. I've been through every square inch of this place these past few months. I wasn't taking any chances of you sneaking away when I came to arrest you. Pace isn't the only one who gets his man. I do, too. I wasn't going to be leaving without you then, and I'm not letting you ditch me now. You won't be leaving me behind, Roni. Not today, and not ever."

Roni cringed at the forceful tone in Ethan's voice. She didn't feel threatened, but she also didn't know this side of him. Up until now, his compliance had preceded him. But it had been a farce. He wasn't being compliant at all. As he'd said, he'd been leading this show the whole time, letting her believe she had been the master of ceremonies.

"Why do I get the feeling I'm being taken in?" she asked from in front of him.

Ethan guided her from the center of her back. His hand warmed her and didn't come across as anything but helpful. The helping hand of her sidekick, except he wasn't her sidekick after all.

The passage narrowed, but even in the pitch-dark, she knew she would come out in the garage and walked with no fear.

Just concern.

"Well? Are you arresting me?" she asked.

A light flashed a few feet ahead, halting her steps. Before she could adjust her eyes, Ethan filled the tight space before her with his frame. He blocked her view from the person who had turned on the beam.

"Stand back," Ethan warned with a voice so menacing *she* pushed into the wooden walls to follow his order. Where was her kind, protective Ethan she'd come to know and…care about? "State your name, or I shoot," Ethan said. Roni didn't get that kind feeling now.

But the way his arm kept her behind him, she did get the protective feeling. That much hadn't changed. Knowing he stood before her calmed her even in the presence of someone who meant to harm her.

"You have to ask? Who else knows about these passages but us?"

"Pace!" Ethan said and feigned back. "You're alive!"

Roni felt Ethan's tensed body relax in an instant. The air rushed out from his lungs on a whoosh. She was glad to know his friend hadn't been in that helicopter. That Ethan hadn't lost someone important to him.

Even if the guy held a gun on her now.

"Where have you been?" Ethan asked. "I've been trying to call you all night."

"There's a shoot-out going on out there, in case you missed it. Ramsey's men are coming out of their wormholes to retaliate. Thanks to you the whole organization is coming apart at their sweat-shop seams, but that's also made a lot of people mad."

"Have you called in all teams?"

"They're all here, and so is this little town's finest. It's like the O.K. Corral out there. If it's all the same to you, I'd like to wrap this up tonight."

"I'd like nothing more, believe me."

Metal jangled from somewhere beyond the light. "Good. Then move aside so I can cuff Miss Spencer," Pace said.

Ethan's relaxed body tensed again. "I can't let you do that, Pace. She's been set up. She's innocent in all matters."

"You have proof of this?"

"No, but Ramsey is sure to squawk."

"Ramsey's MIA. We're hoping he was in the helicopter but won't know until the bodies can be identified. You got anything else?"

At Ethan's lack of response, the light grew brighter with every step Pace took toward them.

"Veronica Spencer, you are under arrest."

The next moment, the light flew up and off to a corner where it rocked back and forth until it came to a stop. It offered only a shred of illumination to the two men gripping each other's arms in a battle of equal strengths.

"Run!" Ethan said, his voice sounding strained.

"No, Ethan. I'll go willingly. I don't want you doing this for me. We'll both be arrested."

"I'd listen to her if I were you," Pace warned.

"So you can get your man? You're wrong about her."

The shadow of a head-butt had Roni reaching to a grunting Ethan.

Pace pushed Ethan back. "I'm not walking out without her. And she doesn't even have to be alive."

Roni shrank away at Pace's statement. The man would gun her down? She wasn't even armed. At least not anymore.

Roni thought of running back up to the foyer and grabbing the gun left there, but there was no time and Ethan needed her help.

He had a gun on him, but where?

She stepped up behind him and touched his back.

"Roni!" Ethan yelled. "Go!"

Her hand touched the weapon. The same weapon he had used to show her how to shoot. But pretending to shoot was not the same as actually taking aim and pulling the trigger.

And she could never kill someone, a federal agent or not.

Roni snatched the gun from Ethan's waistband and cocked it as he'd shown her. The clicking sound echoed in the small cavernous passage.

"Innocent, is she?" Pace said in his struggled stance. "I won't be waiting to find out."

With that, Ethan came flying back at her. She tried to sidestep him but he collided into her, sending her in the direction of the door.

A gunshot blasted off right near her ear. Her eardrums burned with resonating and unrelenting pain.

Roni dropped to the floor, her hands covered her ears, her own gun gone in her agony. Not again, her mind screamed as she focused on where she was hit. If she was hit. *Please, God. I'm not strong enough to fight the pain again.*

Hands grabbed her wrist and pulled it behind her before she could ascertain her condition.

Would Pace be bringing her out dead after all?

SIXTEEN

Ethan knew Pace had to be fuming. His boss never missed his mark. Any second, Ethan expected him to retaliate for his shot gone awry. He expected his boss to put aside their lifelong friendship and make him pay for moving the target.

Except the target had been Roni.

The thought soured Ethan's stomach, and not just because it was proof that his old friend had lost all sense of reasoning and ethics, but because the thought of Roni taking Pace's bullet made him ill.

He'd pushed her out of the way knowing full well he could expect the lead to find him, but the alternative couldn't happen. If she died it would be his fault. If she died he…he pushed the thought away. Somehow he knew it would be worse than the last time he nearly lost his charge.

This time it would be personal.

He'd crossed the line in his responsibilities. No

doubt about it. He would have to straighten himself out once he brought Roni to safety.

Ethan raised his gun, the same gun he'd lifted off Roni when he'd moved her from the bullet's path. It was an easy pinch. He would have to teach her how to hold her weapon firmly. But first he had to get her out of here.

"Put your gun down, Agent," Pace instructed. "Put it down now, and I'll chock this up to a minor misunderstanding."

"Do what you have to, Pace, but I'm still leaving here with Roni." Ethan backed away with Roni's wrist still in his hand. He guided her to go ahead of him through the door while he kept his gun on Pace. Never did he think he would find himself in this situation.

The angry shadows on Pace's face played out his own shock.

"You're making a big mistake, Ethan. One word from me and you're done. You'll be back in the alleys of the neighborhood."

Ethan pushed through the door without a response. There really wasn't anything else to say to his old friend. Ethan had made his decision. The fallout would be his problem.

The door closed between him and Pace, but not before Pace shouted, "It's a trap. And you're playing right into her hands!"

Ethan shot a glance at Roni's face at Pace's accusation, but without the light, he couldn't make

out any true features. It didn't matter. Pace wa
wrong about Roni, and Ethan would prove it..
or die trying.

"You shouldn't have done that, Ethan. You'
regret it forever," Roni called from behind wher
he pulled her along the rows of cars in her glass
enclosed garage. A real showroom. He'd scope
the collection out when he'd surveyed the hom
months ago.

Ethan led her to the safe that held the keys t
each of the vehicles. "What I would have regre
ted forever is if he had found his mark. Now g
the key to the Lotus. It's the closest one to th
garage doors. We're going for a ride."

When she withdrew the key to pass over t
him, he turned away without it. "You're drivin;
And hold nothing back."

"Nothing? Do you trust me with your life?"

"You have to ask? I just threatened to shoo
my boss for you. Of course I trust you. I believ
you, and I trust you. And I know Pace is wron
about you. You have no plans to entrap me. Th
man has gone off the deep end with his paranoi
He only sees what he wants to see. I'm going
show him the truth."

"And that is?"

Ethan closed the passenger side door an
locked gazes with her. "You're the real thin;
Roni. You keep nothing hidden and you hav
nothing to hide."

As he knew she would, Roni reached for her scarf. He grabbed her hand before she made contact. "I meant what I said. You have nothing to hide. Nothing."

She looked straight ahead, breaking the contact he tried to keep. "Where to?"

"First you'll have to get by the shooters out there. Can you handle that?"

She gave a firm nod. "Avoiding the line of fire is my expertise, remember?"

"Then break us out of here."

Roni revved the engine and prepared to drive. "Stay low. I'm not opening the door."

"Then how do you plan to drive out?"

She smiled and floored the gas…straight out the glass windows. Ethan didn't have time to come to grips with Roni's decision. One minute all was quiet and safe, the next he was airborne in the midst of millions of shattering glass shards. He had to question the full trust he'd just given Roni—but only for a second, because as soon as they hit the driveway, the car shook with the pummeling of bullets. The rear window blew in on them.

"Get down!" he yelled as he reached out for Roni.

Roni crouched low in the driver's seat but kept her hands on the wheel and gearshift. She pressed the clutch with her foot and brought the car to its

next gear. Within moments the car cleared thei
shooters and approached the base of the twisting driveway.

"Right or left?" She said her first words to
Ethan's ashen face. It quickly dawned on her tha
he might have been hurt. Panic rushed in as she
surveyed him from head to toe. "Were you hit?"

"No." He sagged back against his headrest
"But I thought…I thought you…"

Their eyes met and held. Slowly, she lifted he
hand from the steering wheel and touched hi
trembling one.

"Hey, you're really shaken up. Do shoot-out
typically do this to you?"

"Never."

His breathing slowed as his hand turned to
take hers fully. With a squeeze, he said, "Drive
It won't be long before we have company."

Roni let his partial confession go and took
left. It would be the long route down the moun
tain, but she thought her followers would thin
she took the fastest route since this road went u
before it descended. That would be the most logi
cal way, but when her mother and father set ou
with their children twenty-eight years ago, the
took the right and didn't make it ten feet befor
being plowed right over the edge and down int
the ravine. Roni let that be her answer for her d
rection now.

Narrow twisty turns concealed the car, bu

they also slowed them down. Ethan rubbernecked for followers.

"Anyone yet?"

"Not yet. I don't see any bouncing headlights behind the bends either."

"Seems odd they wouldn't break up. I figured they would think I took the right, but it would be shoddy of them not to send someone to the left. Unless…"

"Unless what?"

"Do you think your boss would hold them back from going after us? Like maybe he believed you when you told him I was innocent?"

He huffed. "Just wait for it. They'll be here."

Light beams bounced from behind the bend as if on cue.

"Get ready. I see lights. Can you step on it?"

Roni gave the car more gas, but at the next bend had to slow down again. "I'm sorry. There's just something about driving these mountain roads that has always made me treat them with care. I don't remember going over, but I remember the aftermath, and that's enough to slow me down. The racetrack is different. There I can defy death. But these roads already have me beat. They've already showed me who's boss, and it's not me."

"You're wrong. I've seen you take tighter corners than these roads without hesitation. These roads have not beaten you. Now's your chance to prove that. Drive, Roni."

"You confidence in me is—"

"Earned. I wouldn't have handed you the key otherwise. In fact, I wouldn't trust anyone else to drive this car right now. You have what it takes. Believe it. It's the truth."

"I usually have to fight for words like those."

Ethan turned his head from his watchman position. A strange look cast from his shadowed, dashboard-lit face. "You're not the person I thought you were. Even though I knew about your scars, you were still so far above someone like me, I knew there would never be anything we would have in common. I was wrong. But I didn't know that. And your family and friends probably don't know it either. They look at you and think you don't need anyone. You've got it all together." Ethan looked back out the passenger side mirror and continued in a low voice, "Sometimes people need to see your scars, so they know you're just like them."

Roni felt her lips quiver. She focused on the road, but her hands gripped the wheel so tight, her nails pierced the skin of her palm.

The cabin's silence roared louder than the engine. She thought for sure Ethan would hear her heart thudding in her chest. His words gave her so much to ponder, but part of her was grateful now was not the time. Maybe never.

"Well?" Ethan said. "Are you driving this thing, or aren't you?"

Roni nodded once and attempted to take ownership of the roads. She power-slid into the next bend, easing into the throttle with smooth and steadying efforts. The car's back end barely slid out and with only the slightest screech.

"See? You got this. I knew you could do it."

Roni smiled but approached the next turn with deliberation. Should she ease into the throttle again, or countersteer through the slide? A headset from a spotter would be useful right about now. Someone to tell her what's on the other side of that bend.

She chose the throttle again, and the car responded beautifully. Each successful winding turn emboldened Roni's confidence until she raced into the next curve. The tires emitted a crunching sound, letting her know there was a modicum of grip and traction. The challenge was to find the grip, control the braking, balance the slides and then toss everything out the window with the next turn because the course was constantly changing. But these roads that had always held her past over her relented their power as she increased hers. These roads were no different than any others she had mastered. And she owned plenty all over the world.

"I think you lost them. There's no way they're keeping up," Ethan said and righted himself back into his seat to face forward.

Roni barely heard him over a niggling thought

about her mastering roads all over the world. "You mentioned the FBI has a picture of me and Guerra in Florida together. I was in Miami last winter, testing a course for Jared. Before sending him to an invitational, I typically would drive the course myself to see if he could handle it. I don't remember Guerra, but there's a chance I met him. There were a lot of people there. A lot of them were street racers."

"Was Jared with you?"

"No, he was away on some other business that week. He told me to go and let him know what I thought about the track."

"Did he end up racing there?"

"Funny, because I said no, don't bother. Street racers don't follow the same rules. Any rules really. It didn't feel legit, and I worried for him. But he came down the next day anyway. He was angry and accused me of not having respect for his talent. This was about the time the relationship went south. I just told him, have at it, but don't get yourself killed. I flew home by myself."

"Perhaps he was actually there from the beginning, or at least long enough to snap a picture with you and Guerra shaking hands. If he knew Guerra and knew the man was a criminal, a picture like that could be used as collateral, if he needed it in the future. By the sounds of it, he knew that day was coming."

"And part of me knew it, too." Roni took the

next turn in silence, remembering his cruel actions and words in Florida. "It was so hot that day, and I loosened my scarf. He said there were cameras all over the place and told me to cover myself. Nobody wants to lose their lunch."

Ethan whistled a slow retort. "I am so glad you cut that man off."

A beam of light projected into the night from around the next bend in front of them.

"Ethan! They're coming at us now. But how?"

"Maybe it's not anyone but an innocent driver out for an early-morning drive."

"They would have to be really lost. This road follows the ridge for miles to an abandoned castle for hikers to climb to. Then it descends down the mountain."

"Could they have come up another way?"

"Um, there're some unpaved roads that could get them up here, but those aren't even on a map. How would Ramsey's men or even the FBI know about them?"

"Would Jared?"

Roni shot Ethan a quick look before gripping the steering wheel tighter. "Yes. I've taken him on a tour of all the private roads on my property. If he was at the house, he would know the way to cut me off at this end. But if it's him, then he must have been hiding out and saw me take the left out of the drive. What do I do? There's no place to turn around here."

The approaching car hooked out from behind the bend. The Lotus's headlights shone on the vehicle.

"That's not my Porsche," she said, but before she could determine the make and model, the car straightened out its wheel and crossed over to her side of the narrow road.

One second, Roni owned the roads, the next she jolted with the bang and crunch of the two cars colliding head-on. The Lotus hurdled off the side of the road and kept moving.

Roni lost sight of the second car as she attempted to bring her car under control. Trees whizzed by as they sped down the incline backward. Images of another crash smashed into her mind's eye. One where the car flipped upside down over and over.

She shook the flashing images from her mind to focus on this car. Roni yanked the wheel to turn the tires for traction, but only managed to slam the passenger side into a tree. Glass shattered. She whipped the wheel back and put the car back into a descent. The car bounced up once, then smashed into a tree from behind and came to a complete stop. That's when she saw Ethan out of the corner of her right eye.

His head slumped forward and hung there, lifeless.

"Ethan!" she screamed, inhaling the sharp cut of smoke at the same time.

Smoke?

Roni's senses hit full-on alert. Where there's smoke there's fire.

But a crane of her neck didn't show any flames. Her nose did pick up the unmistakable scent of gasoline.

Fire was sure to come.

"Ethan, wake up. The car could blow any second." She reached for Ethan's slumped head. Two things occurred at the same moment that made this situation worse.

Her hand touched blood when she lifted Ethan's face. A gash from his forehead pulsed blood out of his body.

But when she shifted her body to reach him, the car swayed as though it was suspended in air, teetering like a seesaw.

Roni retracted into her seat, letting Ethan's head fall back to his chest. Sure enough, the car swayed back

With the darkness outside and her headlights reaching up to the road, Roni couldn't make out exactly how the car teetered. Was she hanging over a cliff? Was the car stuck in a tree? A scan around gave her no answers.

But the mingling odors of smoke and gas and Ethan's blood also told her she couldn't stay here all night.

Roni pulled the latch of the driver's door and slowly eased it open. She peered out without moving her body in any direction. Matted-down leaves were only two feet away.

Roni sighed with the small relief of not being up in a tree, but a look past Ethan's head to the vast stretch of darkness attested to a much worse situation. One move too far that way, and they could go over the edge.

"Ethan." She heard the tears in her voice and swallowed hard when no reply came.

How could he? He was hurt. She had to get him out somehow and stop his bleeding.

Smoke released from the engine, pushing her to move before a plan could be thought out. This whole place could blow long before the car plunged off the cliff.

Slowly, Roni reached to Ethan's belt buckle. She braced the front of him, maneuvering her arm around to his far arm. At the sound of the release, she yanked him to her side of the car.

Groans and creaks echoed all around her, but none came from Ethan. The sickly warped sounds emanated from the swaying car teetering on this precipice.

Ethan's heavy weight stunned her. The thought that he was already dead hadn't entered her mind. This was strong FBI agent Ethan. He'd gone up against men like Guerra and come out clean as a whistle. How could a car crash be his demise?

Another groan filled the car.

Hers.

Roni knew just how deadly car crashes were. A car crash killed her parents. She'd seen car crashes kill race car drivers in an instant, no matter how strong and healthy they were.

But this was different. This felt so different.

She let Ethan's head rest on her shoulder. The slight movement creaked the car again. Roni closed her eyes, knowing her next move to pull him out would have to be her fastest move ever. All those racing accidents she'd avoided never came this close to besting her.

She'd taunted death so many times to claim her after missing its chance years ago. She would have to raise her fist of defiance again, but this time it wasn't just for her. This time she would fight for Ethan.

"Do You hear me, God? I will fight You for him." Tears pooled in her eyes. A lump lodged in her throat, and her next words came out sounding swollen. "I won't let You take him like You took my family. I won't let You take him."

Like so many split-second moves on the track, Roni made this one just as quick and calculated. She stuck one leg out of the car, and on a twist of her body, used all her leg strength to catapult her and Ethan from the car.

Ethan's eyes opened for a brief second, but something that flashed from the interior of the car pulled her attention from him. She landed hard on top of him and quickly disengaged so she wouldn't hurt him more. She also looked back at the car, wondering what she saw.

A man's arm had been reaching in from the other side.

The car let out its loudest groan yet, a long drawn-out noise that morphed through various pitches before it swayed back one last time.

Multiple seconds of silence descended as it fell through the dark night. Blissful but disconcerting silence that ended with the rushing heat of an explosion that clawed its way back to her, reaching high up into the sky. Leaves in the trees crackled as embers ignited them.

Hot flames scorched Roni's eyes as she took the situation in. She threw her body over Ethan's unconscious one, knowing she had to get him away from the heat and growing flames.

She also knew there had been no man on the other side of that car.

Had it been a memory from her first car crash as a child?

Roni couldn't give a moment to dissecting the image she saw. The explosion roaring in front of her would give their location away to her pursuers. They had to be turning their directions to this spot right now. But which one of them would reach them first?

Honestly, it didn't matter.

She dragged Ethan from under his arms, one pull at a time, nearing the roadside with each strenuous movement. At the incline, she had to stop and rest. She cradled him in her arms and dropped her head forward to his. Blood continued to seep from his wound, slow but steady.

Roni looked out to the fire that burned everything in its wake. But not her this time. She reached to her neck and felt the scarf covering her scars from the world. Scars that showed what she'd been though and what she survived. But no one knew all that because she kept them hidden. No one knew but her…and God. To the world, Roni portrayed herself as someone who was in total control. But it was really only God who she wanted to prove this to. Prove that she didn't need Him. He didn't want her when she called out for Him to take her, so she raised her fist to Him and said, "I'll show You. I don't want You either."

But that was her biggest cover-up ever.

Roni knew the only way to no more appearances had to start with her. There could be no more running from the truth. No more shrouding it either, no matter if the world thought she was ugly.

Roni's gaze fell from the flames to Ethan's flickering face. He would have corrected her word choice, using beautiful instead of ugly. She'd heard it on his lips enough times to know it to be true. That was the truth. He'd been telling her over and over, but she closed her ears and eyes to it, thinking if she did, she wouldn't have to accept it.

"I'm beautiful." The words came out on a whisper. "God, I want to believe it, but beauty can't happen as long as the ugliness is kept hidden."

Roni loosened the knot at her neck. She pulled one end of the silk scarf down until the whole tail of fabric bunched in her hand. She brought it behind Ethan's head to grab one end with one hand while she wrapped the material around his head wound with the other. A few revolutions and she tied it off.

"I'm going to get you help, Ethan." She leaned in close to speak to his relaxed face. "Thank you for all you did for me. Thank you for keeping me safe. Thank you for speaking truth to me, even when I scoffed at your words time and time again." She gazed at the lips that had spoken his perfect words to her, the same lips that had kissed her so passionately. He didn't just tell her she was beautiful. He made her feel it, too.

A car engine roared off in the distance. Her first pursuer closed in. Her time with Ethan neared its end.

"I won't ever forget you, Ethan. You changed my life. You opened my eyes and took off my blinders. Help will be here soon. I'll make sure of it. If I can accomplish nothing else, I will make sure you have help."

A car came to an idling stop right behind her.

Roni's eyelids closed for a brief moment of acceptance. She opened them and pressed her lips to Ethan's. He still felt warm, and she let that fact push her forward on her mission. As the saying goes, pretty is as pretty does, and she would live up to Ethan's praise of her by saving him.

Roni lifted her face and stared at him for the last time. He would be forever a part of her heart. "Goodbye, my love," she whispered and gently laid his head back on the leaves. With one push, she stood and turned to meet her ride.

SEVENTEEN

"Goodbye, my love."

Ethan's injured mind heard the words from Roni's lips spoken as if from miles away. She stood in a doorway. He reached out for her, but his hands disappeared into a smoky haze swirling between them. "Roni," he called to her.

Then suddenly she vanished through the door, taking the blinding white light with her.

"No, don't go in there!"

Ethan shot up to go after her, the bright image of his subconscious replaced with the dark reality of the night.

The red taillights of a car sped off down the road and Ethan figured the headlights had been what blinded him. A look around him showed he'd been left behind. He reached for his aching head and felt silk at his fingertips.

Roni's silk scarf.

"Roni," he spoke with a groan of pain.

The car crash. He remembered being driven

off the side of the road. Nothing else. He'd obviously hit his head.

But where was Roni? Did he get thrown out of the car?

Ethan took notice of the fire blazing farther down the embankment. Fear had him pushing up to a crouch, but the world tilted and sent him back to his knees. He denied that Roni was in the flames. She had to have been the one to get him to the road.

But where did she go after that?

Ethan looked in the direction the red taillights had taken. He pulled the image back and this time he understood what he saw driving away.

A Porsche. The car pulling away had been a Porsche. And not just any Porsche, but Roni's Carrera.

She'd left him behind and went with Jared.

But why?

After everything she had learned she knew he would kill her.

An engine roared louder as it approached, and soon more could be heard with sirens.

Ethan covered his ears at the mind-splitting pain the high-pitched noises caused. He figured he must have a concussion, if nothing else. He hoped nothing else, because he had to find Roni.

"Ethan? Is that you?"

Ethan recognized his friend's voice but couldn't

make him out with the light from the high beam
behind him.

"Pace! Pace, we have to find Roni. She's i
danger."

Pace let out a sigh as he stepped down the em
bankment. "You've really lost your marbles wit
this one. That girl has done a number on you. I'
cut you some slack this time because of her goo
looks, but seriously, she took you for a ride."

Ethan let Pace lift him by the arm until h
stood. He leaned on his friend because he ha
to, but worked hard to hold his own. Especiall
since he didn't like the way Pace degraded Ron
The dig felt personal. "You don't understand her.

"I think I have a pretty good picture of wh
Roni Spencer is. Let me guess. She left you fo
her ex. At least she bandaged you up. Come on
the ambulance is arriving. I want them to have
look at your head."

"No! We have to go after her."

"Oh, we will. Trust me."

Ethan let himself be led up to the road to th
paramedics. When scissors were brought near hi
head, he held them back. "No, don't cut the scarf

It was an absurd request. He knew it, yet h
couldn't bear to see her scarf cut to shreds, eve
though he never wanted her to wear it again. Bu
right now, it was all he had of her.

Maybe Pace was right. Maybe he had lost h

focus. To have such thoughts about Roni only meant one thing. He had it bad.

No. Not bad. There was nothing bad about her.

"What can I say to make you consider for one moment that Roni was set up?" Ethan asked as the paramedic unraveled the silk from his head. Ethan reached for it before she tossed it in the trash.

With the material in his hand, Pace saw he was going to have to listen to Ethan.

"Well, since my best friend pulled a gun on me tonight and is now holding on to a piece of women's clothing, I suppose I don't have much choice but to hear him out, no matter how demented anything you could say would be."

"Jared Finlay is dangerous. He tried to kill me. Took a shot at me at the gas station."

"Negative. He took a shot at a propane tank, which caused an explosion that crashed the helicopter above. The fire inspector found the bullet holes clear as day once the blaze was put out. He wasn't trying to kill you, although I'm sure he wouldn't have lost any sleep over your dead body. I'm thinking he was trying to free his girlfriend from her pursuers in the helicopter. And it worked."

"His girlfriend? Their relationship is over."

"Says Spencer. Boy, she's been lying to you. When are you going to get that through your dented skull?" Pace reached into his pocket and pulled out his cell phone. "Now you're going to listen to my proof. This is how we knew where to find you and to come with the ambulance."

Pace pulled up an audio file on his phone and lifted it for Ethan to hear.

"911 operator, what is your emergency?"

"This is Veronica Spencer. I was just in an accident with an FBI agent. His name is Ethan Gunn and he's unconscious. I left him on the side of Summit Road right before the trail entrance to the castle. I got him away from the fire. He needs medical attention. He hit his head. Will you send him help?"

"Yes, ma'am, I have crews in the area. They'll be there in a few minutes. Are you able to wave them down?"

"No. I've left the scene. Just please, hurry. I never meant for him to get hurt. This isn't how it was supposed to be."

Click.

"Ma'am? Ma'am, are you still there?"

Pace hit the end button. "So, you want to enlighten me on how Spencer's in so much danger? Because from that message, I'd have to say, you were the one in danger this whole time. You let your guard down and nearly got yourself killed."

"Someone smashed into us. Someone sent us off that road." Ethan jammed his pointer finger in the direction behind Pace.

"I don't doubt it. Spencer has a lot of enemies

But her ex isn't one of them. They must have realized organized crime had better money flow than winning car races. They hooked up with Guerra in Miami, and the rest is history."

"She didn't know Guerra." Ethan wasn't ready to relinquish his faith in Roni yet. There had to be something he wasn't seeing. Something that would make sense of all this.

"She told you that, too?"

Ethan ignored the condescending note in Pace's voice. He closed his eyes to push past the pain to find what he needed to make sense of why Roni would leave him.

"Goodbye, my love." The words from his unconscious state flittered about inside his cranium.

"She must have gone with him, in return for calling for help. For me." Ethan stood up, pushing the paramedics off from doing the final dressing of his wound. "Yeah, that has to be it. I'm going after her." Ethan raced to Pace's car, still parked and idling on the side of the road.

"Get back here, and that's an order. I'm not cutting you any more slack."

"Can't. Sorry, Pace. But she loves me. She left me behind because she loves me. What other proof could you possibly need of her innocence? If she was guilty, she wouldn't have cared about what happened to me."

Ethan reached the driver's door of the unmarked federal car. He got in and was surprised to see Pace get in the passenger side.

"I'm not taking more danger to her. I've brought enough to her already, mainly because of you. I don't want you with me if you're just going to take her out. She's not trafficking anyone, Pace. You can't make her pay for what happened to your sister!"

Pace's eyes flashed anger but quickly looked forward.

Ethan calmed but plowed forward, holding nothing back in this crucial moment. "I think you've been too close to this case for a long time. I'm telling you this as your friend, nothing more. I will never repeat this to anyone else, unless you give me reason to."

"Are you threatening me again? First with your gun, and now with legal action?"

"I just want you to be aware of the choices you have. Stay behind or come with me, but if you come with me, this is a hostage situation, not takedown. So what's your choice?"

Jared Finlay's childhood home felt small and closed in, but the gun held on Roni might have contributed to her claustrophobia. She sat on one of the four kitchenette chairs that squeaked with her every move and gave away any plan of escape. The front door and the back kitchen door couldn't be more than fifteen feet apart, but with

Jared's towering frame blocking both paths, neither were accessible exits. Especially with the gun cocked and ready. She might make it in time to dive behind one of the tattered couches, but they didn't look as if they could fend off any bullets, or support a person, for that matter.

But it wasn't the state of the furniture that concerned Roni. It wasn't the old dilapidated factory house he grew up in either. It was the fact that she knew this was where he was from, and she'd turned a blind eye to his situation.

"I'm sorry, Jared."

Jared angled a look over his shoulder at her, his gun swinging around at her. "What have you done now?"

"I mean for what I did before. I never should have publicly called you out. I didn't have the right to take your livelihood away from you. You're a great driver. I shouldn't have had you blacklisted from the sponsors."

"Good, because you're going to fix that first thing in the morning. Call up your TV crews and do what you have to do to get a press conference."

"I will."

"You will?" Jared's nervous expression doubled. He retraced his steps to the front windows for nearly the hundredth time. "Is this a trick? Is your FBI man out there ready to ambush me? Did you lie to me when I allowed you to make that 911 call? You said he was unconscious."

Pain shot to Roni's heart. She grabbed at her blouse with a fisted hand. "No, he's not out there. Hopefully, he's being treated and…" She swallowed hard. "I pray God is caring for him."

"God? I thought that was one thing we agreed on. We're in this world on our own. Take what you can when you can."

"We were wrong, Jared. God does care. He cared about freeing Maddie."

"Who?"

"Maddie. She was one of Ramsey's bought servants. God freed her because He really does care. And He cares about Ethan, too. He cared about my parents, and He cared about my burns. Nothing is hidden from Him. He sees all, and He makes all things beautiful in their time. But it's in *their* time, not ours. That's what I never understood. I screamed at Him to heal me or kill me, but it wasn't my time for either."

Jared curled his lip at the sight of her exposed neck. She knew her scars still disgusted him, but now she also knew that was his problem, not hers.

"It's who I am, Jared. I can't change the way I look. But it's also *not* who I am." She patted her chest. "God cares about the beauty in here, and tonight, I have never felt more beautiful. He's changing me, and I have Ethan and Maddie to thank for that. Ethan always saw it, and Maddie—" Roni smiled "—Maddie never stopped praying for it. She prayed for me, even when her own life was in bondage. And, Jared, I'm going to start praying for you."

"Save it. I don't believe a word you're saying. You've always been out for yourself, wanting the world to know it was all you. *I* was the one behind the wheel!"

"And I already told you I will rescind what I said."

"Why?"

"Because I don't want to be out for myself anymore. I want to go after the things God has planned for me. Cora always said He had great plans for me, but I didn't want to hear it. Now that I'm listening again, I think He wants me to open my home as a safe house for trafficked women. It's the perfect place and has everything it needs to give these scared and hurting women a place to feel secure and free. If Maddie is agreeable, I want to do this."

"What about your racing school?" Jared peered out the window, pointing his gun to the ceiling.

Roni had thought her words would have calmed him, but he seemed just as nervous.

"I suppose that was something I thought was best for me, and I'll be sad to let it go, but I only want to do what God wants me to from now on. I'm serious about this, and my past can no longer define me. From now on I want to reflect His goodness in my life. It all makes sense to me now. I've been racing toward death since the car crash, doing whatever I could to show God I didn't need Him. That if He didn't take me then, He would never take me. It was one of the many lies I believed. My life of appearances is over. From now on, it's nothing but truth."

Roni hiked her chin to expose her neck more fully and to show she meant it.

He sneered again and looked away, back out the window. "You'll change your mind, and that's the truth."

"Why?" Roni squinted in confusion. "What have you done, Jared? Who are you actually waiting for? I thought you were watching for the authorities, but something tells me that's not the case. Is it Guerra? You were the one who made a deal with him to set me up, and now you're afraid he's going to come collecting and hold you responsible for the demise of the Boss?"

"The man would thank me for the demise of the Boss. Now Guerra's in charge."

"Of a dismantled organization."

Jared shook his head. "He'll just start another one. Don't be so naive, Roni."

Roni sobered. "I'm not, Jared. I understand the battle of trafficking humans is daunting, but that doesn't mean we should do nothing. That we should turn a blind eye to the fact that it's happening right under our noses, in our hometowns and cities. We need to be aware and watchful, and we need to speak up when we see something that doesn't look right. There are many organizations that will tell us how to recognize the signs and to know what to look for, and I hope I can be one of them someday."

Jared frowned and turned back to the window, barely listening.

Roni leaned back in her chair, the creak long and mimicking her unease. "So, if you're not waiting for Guerra, why do you have me here at gunpoint?"

"I'm not holding a gun on you. I'm protecting you from someone who wants you dead. I may not think too highly of you, but I never wanted you dead...or sold. I just wanted you to lose everything, to know what it felt like to be dirt-poor. Guerra promised me you would feel the pain of losing everything. That's all I wanted. Now I'm trying to fix this. To end this tonight before it's too late for her."

"Her? Who are you talking about? Who wants me dead? What are you trying to fix?" The back kitchen door slammed, and Roni whipped around. A face with mangled hatred stared at her from behind a gun's black barrel. It had Roni wishing it was Guerra standing there. He'd never looked at her with such revulsion. Now she knew this was never about business.

This was personal.

EIGHTEEN

"How are you still alive? I saw that car explode!" The words shook from Tanya Finlay's snarled lips. "I should have put a bullet in you a year ago and skipped this whole setup. I should've known not to depend on others for *anything*!"

Roni jerked back in her chair as far as she could lean. The chair screamed for her, while her mind raced with what this all meant. Her fingers curled around her seat to keep her steady. She could show no fear.

"You're the one who wants me dead?" she said slowly. To Jared, she said, "And you knew. Did you ever love me, or was it always just a ploy to get ahead?"

Jared scoffed. "Oh, please, you never loved me. You loved that you made me a success. You were already pulling away from the relationship before Miami. I knew the breakup was coming. I had to have something over you."

"That's not true. I wanted to see the man Cora

told me was inside of you. I trusted her when she said you were a man of worth."

"Worth!" Tanya snarled. "Look around you. Does it look like we have two pennies to rub together? We have *nothing*. All you had to do was say, 'I do.' Then we would finally have our portion. We would have even more than Cora, finally."

"So, I wasn't your first sale, then," Roni shot back. "You sold your son first."

Confirmation flickered on Jared's face, but he said, "She only did what she thought was best for me."

"Best for you? Maddie's mom thought she was doing what was best for her, too. A lie whispered. Appearances made. People believe what they want to. Even if the reality is it will bring more strife to their loved one. A life of being a slave to your decisions and of having no identity anymore. That's not what's best for you."

"Stop it!" Tanya screamed and waved her gun, reminding Roni she came to use it.

"You're going to be caught, Tanya. Guerra and his men will squawk when they're arrested. The authorities will find you. They'll know you orchestrated everything, and they'll come get you. That's the truth. It's all over now."

"We'll be long gone before they do."

"You won't get far with your two pennies," Roni pointed out.

Tanya laughed, a sick maniacal sound. "Why do you think I took Cora's offer to hide in your home?" Tanya lifted a small but hefty duffel bag. "I knew you had an emergency stash in that safe room of yours. Your emergency stash is more money than I've seen in my whole life. Once I was inside, it was easy to get what I came for... and have a little fun with you."

The pictures.

Roni didn't respond. She refused to give the woman the time of day. "Cora wouldn't have let you walk out with my money," she said.

Tanya feigned a look around the room. "Well, now, you don't see Cora, do you?"

Roni's lungs inhaled and squeezed tight. "What did you do to her? Your *sister*?"

"My sister wore out her purpose. She stopped giving me anything but her *prayers*." The word was clearly distasteful to Tanya's lips, but to Roni it opened her lungs with peace.

"I wish I realized sooner that her prayers were the best thing she ever did for me. That goes the same for you, Tanya. Please tell me you didn't kill her."

"I'm done talking. You should have been dead the night you went out to the track. Guerra knew you would be coming. Jared arranged for him to use the garage as a chop shop, and I waited until you found out. Only, to the public eye, it would look like you arranged it and got caught up in a world of crime. Racing queen burns herself this time, and dies."

Dies.

Roni knew she would have died immediately that night at the garage by Guerra's hands if not for Ethan stepping in and saving her. He may have believed her to be guilty of all the crimes Jared set her up to take the fall for, but the undercover FBI agent sent to take her in put his life on the line for her that night.

And every moment since.

Somehow Ethan Gunn had melted her plastic exterior with the slow burn of his warmth, and she never even realized love could do that.

Love.

All this time, Ethan was loving her. Did he know that's what his actions were? In these final moments of life, she held on to the belief that he did love her. She only wished she could have told him she loved him, too.

A gun clicked, and Roni snapped to attention, raising her chin in defiance.

Only this gun was Jared's, and he wasn't aiming it at her. Jared pointed his gun at his mother.

"This ends here, Mom."

Then Jared did something Roni wouldn't have ever believed possible of him. He stepped in front of the table, blocking his mother's aim with his own body.

"No more lies," Jared said. "You don't want

Roni dead for me. You want her dead because o
the hatred you have for your own life. Killing he
won't change that fact."

"I say it will," Tanya said and charged at he
son with a war cry that sent enough electricit
up Roni's spine to send her chair to the floor i
the same moment a gun exploded.

Ethan pulled the unmarked car up to Tany
Finlay's darkened row house. A cacophony o
dog barks put him on alert. But lights from th
neighbors' homes flicking on one by one told hir
something just went down around here.

"They're in the house," he stated to Pace sti
sitting beside him. "Get backup here, and mak
sure these people stay inside their homes. An
down. We don't need stray bullets finding ta
gets. I'm going in."

Pace shot an arm out to stop him. "You're n
to go anywhere until backup arrives. Don't forg
I'm in charge still. I give the orders."

"Not this time, Pace." Ethan shook off his ho
and jumped from the car. Pace opened the pa
senger door, but Ethan had already made it pa
the shrubs at the end of the concrete walkway.

Suddenly a force connecting with his back se
him sprawling to the hard earth.

"Pace! I will hurt you," he shouted as he push
himself up on one hand and tightened his ho
on his gun.

"I've been wanting to do this for a long time, muchacho." A familiar voice spoke beside Ethan's ear.

Guerra.

A foot slammed down on Ethan's wrist, and one look up showed Ramsey, alive and well.

"We meet again, Gunn."

One look over his shoulder showed Pace on the ground grabbing his own head.

They'd been ambushed as soon as they exited the car. Two against two, and he and Pace were already down.

Ramsey kicked Ethan's weapon away, then kicked him in the face before he could react. Blood spurted out from one of the pained places on his head. Guerra used the moment to haul Ethan up by the arms for another hit by Ramsey. Except the only grunt came from Ramsey himself when Pace barreled at him full force. The two men hit the ground and rolled, and Ethan didn't wait to see what else happened. He had his own fight to deal with, one that had been in the making for a year.

A year ago, it had been about the investigation. Now it was about getting past the obstacle that stood in the way of rescuing Roni. There would be no joy in this fight. The joy would come when he had Roni safe in his arms.

Ethan let that fact drive his fists into Guerra's chest as he went after his joy.

Punches and the sounds of splitting flesh could be heard from both sets of men, but soon one set slowed down and disappeared, leaving Ethan and Guerra the only two men left standing.

Barely.

Ethan's legs gave out beneath him as he took another swing at Guerra, but his hand met only air. Ethan's knees hit dirt and suddenly Guerra flashed a knife above his head. Ethan wasn't surprised. He knew Guerra always carried his weapon of choice on him. He was only surprised that Guerra waited this long to bring it out. It meant he was done playing.

Ethan rolled to his back and kicked up with his legs. The heels of his boots connected with Guerra's gut and bent him sideways. He swept his legs vertical, taking Guerra down to the ground with him.

An even playing field.

He made a grasp for the knife inches from his face, but Guerra whisked it away and rolled.

Suddenly a set of high beams ensconced their makeshift arena, exposing them for all to see in the early dawn of day. Guerra paused, then jumped to his feet to bolt. Ethan moved to go after him but saw instantly he'd made the wrong move.

Guerra's knife left his hand like a flying dart coming in for a bull's-eye on Ethan's forehead.

Ethan paused a millisecond too long before he

fell to his right. Hot, searing pain ripped through the flesh at his shoulder.

He reached for the knife but found it had taken off a layer of skin and kept sailing. The blade protruded from the dirt behind him, shaking with the impact of its flight.

A turn of his head found Guerra raising his fists above Ethan's head for a final death blow.

"I should have killed the Spencer woman like I was paid to do in the beginning," Guerra snarled. "But rest easy, muchacho. She'll be next."

Then two shots echoed through the night and Guerra froze. His face questioned the situation before the growing blood pulsing out of his chest made all things clear.

Guerra fell to the ground in a heap.

Pace lay behind him, his arm raised with a smoking gun. He dropped it in exhaustion.

"I only shot once," he managed to say before dropping his head back to the ground.

Ethan understood instantly what Pace meant. If he only shot once, then the other blast came from inside the house.

Ethan pulled himself to his knees. He had to get inside, but his blood loss and most likely broken ribs slowed him down. Still, he pushed through and made it to the side door, an arm wrapped around his torso.

A woman's wail cried out through the flapping screen door, stopping him in his tracks. It sounded like a cornered animal, and cornered animals had a way of attacking outright. But Ron needed him.

No, he checked himself. He needed her. His life of going solo wasn't enough. That was the lie he'd always told himself because Ethan Rhodes was a nobody.

"You are going to pay for this!" the wailing woman screamed out.

Ethan turned the knob slowly and silently. Ethan Rhodes may be a nobody, but Ethan Gunn wasn't. And if he died today as Ethan Gunn, then he would die a somebody. He would die knowing Roni lived and her dreams would come true.

NINETEEN

Roni's hands shook in front of her, the sight of blood on them halting full breaths from reaching her lungs. So much blood, but not a drop of it hers.

At the sound of the second gunshot, Roni had watched Jared fall to the floor beside the kitchenette table, two feet from her hiding place beneath. At first the shock stunned her immobile. Jared lay close, groaning and grabbing his stomach. Without thinking of the consequence, Roni crawled out to staunch the bleeding. Without her scarf, she grabbed the tablecloth off the table and found his wound.

"Help me save Jared!" she had cried out.

The answer was a gun in her face, its dark barrel menacing and lethal.

"Tanya, Jared needs help. Let me help him," Roni said at the same time she backed her body into the living room portion of the small room.

One of the two tattered sofas was her best shield, at least better than an open range.

"You had your chance to help him, and you failed. Now you'll pay for killing him." Tanya closed in.

"But he's not dead," Roni reasoned and dived behind the closest sofa.

Tanya wailed, a sickening sound of grief and lost reality, and Roni knew she wasn't getting out alive. The blood on her hands would soon be mixed with her own.

The front door swung wide, and hope soared through Roni. It was an absurd thought, but Ethan filled her mind. Was it him here to save her?

But it couldn't be. He was hopefully at the hospital by now being treated for his own wounds.

So then, who had just opened the door?

Roni shimmied along the back of the sofa, but the sound of voices stopped her cold.

"Tanya, you must stop this right now."

Cora.

"Get out of here, Cora," Tanya yelled. "I have no more need of you either."

"I won't let you kill Roni. She's a daughter to me, and I won't let you take her."

Roni swallowed at Cora's confession. Her heart ached to hold her, but Roni knew that was her own selfish need to hold on to Cora for dear life and not let her live her own life. Cora needed to get out of here and be free. And Roni couldn't let the woman be her life preserver anymore. It was time to take the step to stand on her own and meet her adversary first. Just as Ethan had taught her. Be the one to make the first move.

Roni stood before she could change her mind. She jumped over the sofa and threw herself in the air at Tanya. But once in the air, her mind computed all that transpired around her in fractions of airborne seconds.

Ethan was also in the air, but coming at her in the opposite direction.

Tanya fired her weapon.

Roni collided into her in the same moment Ethan collided into Cora.

Armed men and women stormed through every opening at once and tore Roni off Tanya, only to relieve her of her gun and cuff her facedown on the floor, someone's knee pressed into her back.

Roni scrambled back, looking for Cora in the mayhem. A crowd of emergency personnel encircled someone on the floor. Was Cora hurt? Had the bullet found its target?

Suddenly arms engulfed her from behind, and Roni turned to find Cora. The woman's arms never felt so frail, and Roni gratefully accepted a wool blanket from them. In a daze, she allowed someone to escort them to the front door and out of the craziness, but Roni's feet tripped over themselves as she computed more fully what was happening.

"Where's Ethan? I saw Ethan. Where is he?"

Roni gave the two groups of first responders working diligently on their patients her attention. One she knew to be Jared.

Her feet moved to the second.

"Roni, you need to leave."

She turned to see the person who had draped the blanket over her. Chief Sylvie stood four inches below her, but Sylvie's shorter stature didn't undermine the authority in her voice.

Roni knew these row houses were what Sylvie called home, too. She was a single mom, raising a son by herself, but something happened after she had her son. Unlike Tanya, she didn't wallow in her circumstances and point fingers. She didn't guilt family and friends into supporting her. Sylvie put herself through school and the police academy. She worked her way up to chief of police for her town.

Two women in similar circumstances. Two outcomes to show proof of a better way.

Paramedics carried a stretcher through the front door.

"This one needs to go first. He's bleeding out." A paramedic spoke and Roni finally saw Ethan at the man's feet.

They transported Ethan over to the cot, and Roni inhaled at the sight. His face paled to near white. She stepped forward, but Sylvie restrained her with a tight hold on her forearm.

As though Ethan knew she stood by, he opened his eyes with a few forced flickers. Their gazes latched as his head was fitted securely in the hold to stabilize him.

"Why?" The word spilled from Roni's mouth. Of all the things she wanted to tell him, she couldn't fathom why she said that.

Ethan closed his eyes but quickly opened them. "You can't…lose Cora. She's your chosen family." A flicker of a smile twitched his lips, and she knew he did this for her. Not only would he take a bullet for her, but that carried over to the people she loved. He knew what losing Cora would do to her.

But losing him had her feeling as if she was standing back on that precipice again, teetering on the edge of the gorge.

The paramedics whisked the stretcher out through the door. Roni chased them. She needed to tell Ethan how she felt about him.

At the back of the ambulance, she raced up to the side of the stretcher as they prepared to push it in. She was able to touch a finger to Ethan's arm. His eyes flicked open again, but this time life eluded them. Their glassy, near-vacant stare startled her and pushed her to say what she needed to before she was too late.

"I—"

"You're safe now," he rushed out, cutting her off. His eyes closed as the paramedics pushed the stretcher inside. The doors slammed on her, and the lights flashed and sirens blared.

Roni stood amid the chaotic fallout of all she'd been through, ending here in Tanya's front yard. She stood alone with a blanket hanging over her shoulders.

The ambulance disappeared around the corner at the end of the street. More of them pulled out with the other injured people. Police cordoned off the area from the onlookers of the neighborhood, many of whom worked for her at the track. Most had never seen her scars. Did they see them now under the rising sun? There would be a lot for everyone to get used to seeing, she thought. Once the truth was out, there would be no more covering it up. Instead the truth would strengthen people to stand against the ugliness of the world. Bring it out of the darkness and into the light where God makes all things beautiful.

Roni swiped at tears spilling down her cheeks. Ethan had left his mark on her, but it was nothing compared to the one God was working in her. He was marking her as His. She stood exposed in the light, but for the first time in her life it didn't scare her.

She hoped the people of her town would see God's mark over the ones on her neck, but she also hoped her scars would actually welcome people around her, because scars were something everyone had in common.

Just like Ethan said earlier. Scars gave people a common ground to meet each other at. They allowed people to welcome each other with open arms and no judgment, because everyone had them.

Roni turned for Cora's arms…but found her already in Uncle Clay's. Roni startled at the sight, but quickly checked herself.

No more appearances. Only the truth.

She took slow but purposeful steps toward the two people who'd raised her but kept separate lives out of respect for her.

"I'm sorry I never realized," she said, causing Cora's head to lift from Uncle Clay's chest. "Maybe I did, but it was just another thing I turned a blind eye to. If I ignored it, it didn't really exist. Or, at least it would go away." Roni took a deep breath and accepted the truth. "Consider your resignation accepted, Cora. You're free to go."

Roni turned but was quickly grabbed and swung around into Cora's arms. Arms that all of a sudden had the strength of a mama bear. "One doesn't resign from being someone's mother. That's a lifetime commitment, and it's the one I made twenty-eight years ago. Do you understand, Roni? Retiring never meant leaving you. You're still the daughter of my heart and always will be."

Roni looked to Uncle Clay. His sheepish smile

spoke volumes of the wedge between them. She didn't know how that would ever be fixed or if she wanted it to be. But if Cora loved him, Roni would try.

"I remembered something from the car crash," she told her uncle. The man's arm from the crash filled her mind. At his nod, she continued, "There was a man at the scene. When Wade pulled me out in one direction, a man pulled Luke out through the other rear door."

"That's it? Do you remember anything else?"

"No, but I know now for sure that Luke's alive. And if you say you are truly sorry for the pain you've caused us, then let this be a way for you to make restitution. Help me find my brother and bring him home."

Uncle Clay nodded once. "Of course. I will do whatever I can to find Luke."

"And I will pray for you both," Cora said.

Roni wrapped her arms around her mom. "Thank you, Cora, for never stopping, even when I demanded you to. God and I have come to an understanding. He does want me, but right now, He wants me right here."

Cora cried out with joy and squeezed tighter. "I am so happy to hear you say that. Stay with Him, Roni. He will never forsake you. He loves you so much. He *is* love."

"Love. Yes, He is. But love came crashing in to

my life in more ways than one this week. I need to get to the hospital and tell Ethan all about it. Uncle Clay—"

"You don't even have to ask. Of course I'll drive you there."

Roni followed her uncle and Cora to the car, stopping off to let Chief Sylvie know that's where she would be.

The twenty-minute drive felt like an eternity, but she prayed nonstop for Ethan's care and healing. The paramedics had been on the scene, and she let that push her to stay positive about his well-being. She envisioned herself by his bedside when he woke up, and then she would lay out every truth there was between them. The first being she loved him.

The car pulled up to the ER entrance, and Roni jumped out before it was put in Park. She ran through the double doors and saw a small line at the reception desk.

A nurse in pink scrubs took people's names. She had big round arms that looked as though they could take you down or lift you up, whatever a patient needed at the time.

Finally, it was Roni's turn, and she rushed out her words so fast the nurse didn't understand. "No, I said, Ethan Gunn. He was just brought in with a gunshot wound."

The nurse looked at her chart, a puzzled expression twisting her lips. With a shake of her head, she said, "Sorry, dear, no one here by that name."

"How about Jared Finlay?" Roni asked, thinking maybe she was at the wrong hospital.

The nurse nodded. "Finlay is under police custody. You can't see him. But there is no Ethan Gunn."

Roni stepped away, dazed. The full waiting room of various-aged patients stared at her as she circled the room. Her heart rate and breathing picked up as she turned and saw Cora walk through the doors.

"Roni, what is it? You look so pale." Cora raced to her and took her in her arms.

"Ethan. I have no way of finding him. I don't even know his real name. Oh, Cora, what if he dies? I never told him…"

Roni's uncle went to the front desk and spoke quietly to the nurse. His solemn return face didn't encourage hope. "She said there was a DOA tonight. The name is confidential, and she can't access it."

Roni let the weight of that information settle around her. The only thing she had left was the truth to deal with. "I have no way of finding out if it was him. He came into my life in a flash, and he left it the same way. I have to know. Cora, I have to know."

"Come on, honey, let's go home and call Chief

Sylvie. Maybe she can help us track some information down."

A bit of hope soared in Roni as Cora nudged her numbed body forward. They walked out into the bright light of a new day, their arms secure around each other, bound not by duty or even blood, but by love.

Roni leaned her head on Cora's shoulder. "Thank you, for always being there for me. Because I think I'm going to need you more than ever before."

Cora pulled her close. "I am always here for you, my sunshine."

TWENTY

Roni stepped through the side door of her track's backlot garage. Her heels clicked on the concrete until she stopped on the spot where Ethan had saved her life over a month ago. The garage had been ransacked for evidence by the FBI, but Roni didn't see the mess. She only saw the image of Ethan standing before her. She tried to hold the vision of his tough, handsome face at the forefront of her mind, but soon his baby blues fuzzed away as had all the other places she'd gone to find him in her memories.

She wondered when she wouldn't be able to pull up an image of his face at all. At least with her parents she had photographs to draw on. With Ethan she had nothing. Nothing to prove he'd ever existed in her life.

The not knowing if he lived or died choked her up the worst. To add to her distress, Sylvie hadn't been able to track down any information about him either. The news reported the death o

Guerra and the prosecution of Lyle Ramsey, but none of them mentioned Ethan at all. How could they not give him credit for his undercover work in the investigation? Even Jared and Tanya earned a blip of airtime for their part in setting her up and Tanya's part in attempting to kill her, but nothing about shooting a federal agent. It was as though Ethan Gunn not only didn't exist in *her* life, he didn't exist at all.

Roni knew she couldn't go about her life in this limbo state, but the dreams that had dominated her every waking moment a month ago seemed to take a backseat now. No one was stopping her from opening her racing school anymore. Her uncle's quest to find Luke had him barely saying two words to anyone. A guilty conscience needing to compensate, perhaps? She knew Uncle Clay was out to make amends with her, but also to be able to look himself in the mirror every day.

And to earn Cora's love, as well.

Roni smiled thinking about her maid.

No, not her maid, she corrected herself. Cora was never a maid. She was family and always would be. And if she accepted Uncle Clay's proposal it would make it official. But Roni didn't need anything official to make it truth. Their love and commitment to each other made them family already. And honestly, Roni couldn't fault Uncle Clay for falling in love with Cora. There was so much to love about her, especially her caring spirit that recognized a person's pain, and then offered them comfort through it all.

It was Cora who made these past few weeks bearable. Cora and Maddie were her strength, a makeshift family who chose Roni as their own and took care of her during this time.

Never would Roni have believed losing Ethan would cause such an unrelenting physical pain.

She closed her eyes and tortured herself again by dragging his image to her mind's eye. He smiled and his baby blues crinkled in their corners. She felt her lips smile at the beautiful sight. Her breathing picked up as though her heart knew this wasn't real, and in any second he would be gone again in a flash. She grappled to make it last longer this time, as close to reality as she could imagine it.

"I thought I would find you here," Ethan said with unmoving lips. Roni imprinted the sound of his voice to memory. "You're even more beautiful than the last time I saw you." His voice was closer this time. She could practically feel his warm breath on her face. She felt tears pool up and stream down her face at his words.

Suddenly a warm touch caressed her neck, and Roni's eyes shot open on a sharp inhale.

"Shh, it's just me."

"Ethan," she whispered. He stood directly in front of her. Or did he? Was this her imagination playing tricks on her, some sort of mirage showing her what she wanted to see?

Except, this wasn't the healthy, rugged Ethan she'd conjured up in her mind. This Ethan was pale and thin, and his eyes had dark smudges beneath them. Her heart wept at the sight before her. He looked like death standing up.

She raised a shaking hand to one of his hollowed cheeks, and his eyes closed at her touch.

"Oh, I have missed you so much," he said. "I never realized how much I needed someone in my life until I lay in a hospital bed with nothing but machines to keep me company. Going the solo route has become lonely…and boring." He smiled with cracked lips and opened his eyes. "I just kept thinking I needed to get back to Norcastle so I could sign up for racing school. Consider me your first student. If you'll have me, that is. I can't pay much." His gaze dropped to her chin.

"Ethan," she whispered again. "You're alive. You're alive?"

He looked back into her eyes and smiled weakly. "Yes, I'm alive."

"I went to the hospital, but they couldn't tell me anything. There wasn't an Ethan Gunn even admitted."

Sadness crossed his face. "Sorry about all the confidential protocol. Ethan Gunn isn't real, sweetie. It's my undercover name. That's some-

thing else I needed to come to grips with while
lay in the hospital. Who I really am."

"They said there was a DOA. I thought it was
you."

"Guerra. I was choppered to another hospita
better equipped to handle my wounds."

"Why didn't you call me?"

"I didn't wake up for days, and after that…"
He swallowed hard. "I wasn't able."

His head showed evidence of stitches. She
dropped her gaze to his chest and wondered
where the bullet had entered. She let her hand
fall over his heart, and he reached to entwine hi
fingers with hers there, over the place he'd been
shot. His gaze locked on hers and said so much

"You should be dead," she whispered.

He flashed her a quick smile. "It wasn't my
time. Apparently, God has other plans for m
right now."

"He has plans for me, too. I'm opening a refug
at my home for trafficked women. I'm calling i
Maddie's House, even though she's fighting m
about it. She'll come around, though. She was th
same way when I told her at Ramsey's I was tak
ing her with me when I broke out. She just need
some time to adjust, but even with the name u
in the air, she's already going to be so beneficia
to the women who come—" Roni halted, realiz
ing she was talking a mile a minute about incor

sequential stuff. Her mind suddenly registered Ethan really stood in front of her. Alive!

And with his mouth opened in astonishment. "Roni, this is amazing, although I don't know why I'm surprised. You go after what you want, and I know you'll succeed. I will say, I think Maddie might want to call it Magdalena's House instead. Ask her. And I could help you with connections at the FBI. I mean if you wanted me to."

"No."

"No?"

"No. You just got out of the hospital. You should sit down."

She turned to find a stool, but a quick flick from his hand that still held her whipped her back around to lips that claimed hers.

At first, Roni jolted at the surprise, but all reason flew to the rafters and she wrapped her arms around his neck. She lifted to her tiptoes to gain even closer access to Ethan's lips. Warm, living lips. His hands fell to her waist where his fingers dug deep to hold on to her just as much as she clung to him. More tears streamed down her cheeks, though she was uncertain of the kind of tears they were. She couldn't exactly say they were tears of joy. A deep fear that Ethan would vanish from her life again in the blink of an eye had her pulling away on a cry.

"Tell me your name right now," she demanded. "I want your real name so if you ever disappear again, I'll have a way to find you. Tell me right now."

He reached for her cheek, but she eluded him by pulling it away. She was serious, and she wanted him to know it.

"It's not that easy, sweetheart. I work under cover, sometimes for years. Only family know my real identity, and we're not close enough for them to even know what I do."

"So, if we were family you could tell me? Like if we were married?"

Ethan smirked and studied her face from top to bottom. "Now, there's an idea. But why would someone as brilliant and driven as you want to marry me? You're going to be a famous racing instructor. You don't need a sidekick tagging along and holding you back."

Roni frowned. "I was wrong. You were never just along for the ride. You were a critical part of the team, and I thank God He put you in my life for however short of a time. Besides, I've decided not to open a racing school. With opening a refuge, I need to let that dream go."

Ethan's eyes darkened and narrowed. "Let it go? Roni, you have so much to share. My whole team is ready to learn all your moves, especially after you left them in your dust so many times. They can't let that happen again. Egos and all. They're ready to sign up for the Roni Rhode School of Racing today."

"Roni Rhodes?" Roni shrank back. "Who's Roni Rhodes?"

His lips twisted into a grin. He leaned in to a breath's distance from her lips again. "You will be...when you marry me."

Roni pulled back even faster than before. "Wait. Are you telling me your real name?"

"Besides asking you to marry me, yes."

"Rhodes is your real name?"

He nodded, but his smile fell from his teasing lips. "Ethan Rhodes, but it's not a name I claim as anything great."

"*Are you kidding me? Are you telling me my name will be Roni Rhodes?*" Her voice rose a few pitches in growing excitement. "I can't think of a more perfect name. The Roni Rhodes School of Racing. I'll be turning drivers away with a name like that."

Ethan laughed, the most joyous sound she'd ever heard. "Well, what do you know? My name is good for something after all. So is that a yes?"

"How could I not open a school now? Of course, it's a yes."

Ethan squeezed his eyes shut with a laugh. "About marrying me, Roni. Will you give me the honor of being your forever sidekick by *marrying* me?"

Roni shook her head.

"No?" His voice cracked. His smile fell from his face.

"No. No, you cannot be my sidekick. No, you will not come along for the ride. God did not mean for you to stay here on this earth to put air in my tires. He put us together to bring us closer to Him as husband and wife. It's not even a partnership. It's a union that can't be broken, and I for one have no intention of going against God's plan for us. You will marry me, but *only* if you agree to be more than a sidekick."

Ethan reached for her waist again and pulled her lips close to his. Tears glittered in his eyes. Eyes that dropped to her lips with borderline desperation.

Roni withheld what he wanted. What he needed. "Well? What's your decision, Rhodes? Are you in, or are you out?"

Ethan swallowed deep and rasped out, "I love you, Roni Spencer. I love you with every part of my being. I love that God saw you were what I needed to be whole." His lips trembled as he caught his breath. "I love that He joined us in our journey when we weren't looking for His help at all. We gave up on Him, but He still chose us. Neither of us have been in the driver's seat this whole way. It's always been Him."

"Always," Roni agreed on a whisper. "With God still in the driver seat, He will lead the way for the rest of our lives. But this also means it's no longer a solo ride. Are you okay with that, Ethan?"

Ethan's eyes fell to her mouth. She had to wonder if he was even listening anymore with his one-track mind. Not that her mind wasn't on the same track, but neither of them could move forward until everything was out in the open.

An inch from her lips, he said, "I'm in, Roni. If you'll have me, I'm all in."

She smiled and dropped her forehead to his on a sigh. "Then kiss me, Ethan Rhodes, and let the rest of our lives start right now."

* * * * *

If you enjoyed this exciting story of suspense and intrigue, pick up the other story in the ROADS TO DANGER *series:* SILENT NIGHT PURSUIT

And look for these other titles by Katy Lee

WARNING SIGNS
GRAVE DANGER
SUNKEN TREASURE
PERMANENT VACANCY

Available now from Love Inspired Suspense!
Find more great reads at
www.LoveInspired.com.

Dear Reader,

Welcome back to the White Mountains of New Hampshire. The state holds a special place in my heart. I have some roots planted there and love returning to the majestic beauty of the place every so often.

This second book in the Roads to Danger series continues the Spencer family saga in their quest for the keys to their past. Roni Spencer's quest for the truth landed her in the darkest of dark places, the world of trafficking. Every year, thousands of people are smuggled in and out of the United States to be sold and never heard from again. Many times it is family who sells them. While this is a truth we find hard to believe, we need to understand the lies presented to the families are leading them to believe a fairy tale for their child. The promise of a better life. This is not the truth, but a covering to deny the ugliness of the crime. There are many websites of organizations set up to inform the public of what to look for and what to take notice of, especially in places of travel, like airports and train stations. I encourage you to become aware and to join Roni, Ethan and Maddie by helping to bring this dark world into the light.

Roni and her brother Wade are on to the final road to their past—discovering the truth of what